# RESORTING TO MURDER

A Clowder Cats Cozy Mystery #1

COURTNEY MCFARLIN

## Author's Note

The Clowder Cats are back! So many readers (myself included!) fell in love with the wild cats that appeared in the Razzy Cat Mystery #11, The Crisis at the Wedding, and I decided they needed their own series.

There was only one problem... They needed a human to help, and I wasn't sure who that was going to be until the end of the next Razzy Cat, #12, The Murder on the Mountain. Shireen "Eden" Brooks has quite the story to tell as she embarks on a new path.

If you haven't read those books, never fear! You'll learn about Eden's backstory, as well as the cats, in this book. However, if you're new to my world of talking cats, reading those two books wouldn't hurt.

This new series will feature some old friends, and a bunch of new characters. I hope you enjoy reading it as much as I enjoyed writing it. I can't wait to see where Eden's adventures will take her.

# Chapter One

I sat in my car, half surprised the tired thing had made it all the way to Golden Hills, Colorado, and glanced at my phone before checking the name of the store where I was parked. Mystic Treasures. Yep, this was the right place. My new friend, Hannah Murphy, texted me the address earlier, but she'd left out a few things. Like what this place was and why we were meeting here.

My fingers gripped the steering wheel as a shuddering breath rippled through my lungs. I'd come a long way since I'd left home, but I never would've thought my path would take me to a place where my mother would pitch a fit and likely order an exorcism.

I watched as a beautiful red-haired woman walked outside. Her long, flowing skirt swayed in the breeze and I shivered in sympathy. You wouldn't catch me wearing something like that in the dead of winter, but to each their own. I pulled the sleeves of my sweater down further on my hands and took another deep breath.

The woman made eye contact with me and I felt as if my soul had been laid bare. Her warm smile surprised me and she waved at me, motioning to join her. Well, here goes nothing. Besides, the store was most likely heated, which was yards better than sitting here in my car freezing. My car door made a strangled screech that somehow reminded me of one of my sisters as I forced it open. Closing it carefully didn't make any difference. It still sounded awful. I winced and walked over to where the woman was standing.

"Shireen?"

"That's me. Are you Anastasia Aspen? Hannah Murphy asked me to meet her here."

"I am, dear. Please, come inside, you must be freezing. I felt you out here and figured I'd better come get you."

She felt me? I blinked before walking inside. I barely had time to register the smell of incense before a furry bundle smacked me in the chest. My arms automatically gripped what I quickly figured out was a cat, thanks in a large part to the loud purring sound coming out of it.

"Callie, I've told you about this," Anastasia said, closing the door behind her. "You can't just throw yourself at people. What if Shireen didn't like cats?"

The cat in my arms gave a little chirp and looked into my face, kneading my coat gently with her little paws. Who on earth couldn't love this adorable calico cat? I freed my hand and stroked her head.

"She's fine. I love cats. That's so cool you bring her to work with you."

"She's normally very well behaved," Anastasia said, the love clear in her voice. "My other helper, Kari, is out today. Hannah texted and said she was running behind. There was something she needed to grab, but she's on her way."

Callie chirped again and performed a flying leap out of my arms before I knew what happened.

"No worries. Is she okay?" I asked, glancing down at the cat as she took off down an aisle.

"She does that. She's at that age where they have boundless energy."

I nodded and glanced around the store. Everywhere I looked, I saw something that would've given my mother palpitations. It had been a few years since I'd left the insulated community where I'd grown up, but some feelings were hard to break. Anastasia watched me closely before putting a hand on my arm. She flinched slightly before breaking into a warm smile.

"Don't worry, dear. There's nothing dark inside this place. Never forget that items are just items, no matter what you've been told. Only things you give power to can hold power over you."

"I'm sorry. I wasn't judging you or anything. Honest. It's just..."

"You've had no experience with the things you see here. It's fine. Would you like to walk around? I need to get some tea ready."

I wasn't sure how she knew I needed space, but I nodded gratefully. I heard a soft jingling of bells as she walked away, and I was half convinced I'd met a fairy creature instead of a woman. Something brushed my leg, and I looked down into the mottled face of Callie.

She made eye contact before walking off a few steps and turning around to face me. She crossed the distance again and sat in front of me, looking at me expectantly. I smiled and bent down to pet her fuzzy head.

"You want me to follow you? Okay, cat. Lead the way."

She chirped and started walking, leading me through the aisles. Somehow, her presence made the crystals and herbs seem less scary. She stopped in front of a display of stones and looked at me, her brilliant eyes intent.

"Callie, I swear you're trying to tell me something, but I'm not sure what it is."

I'd just started reading the cards in front of the baskets when a soft bell sounded. I turned in time to see Callie streaking towards the door and spotted Hannah, loaded down with bags. I rushed over to help.

"Shireen! You're here. I'm so sorry I'm late. Hi, Callie. Yes, you sweet thing. Please don't jump up. I'd catch you, but my arms are full."

I grabbed a bag as Hannah shot me a grateful smile.

"Here, let me help you. Oh! You brought cats! Is this Razzy?"

I peered into the bag I was holding and spotted a familiar set of blue eyes. Callie yowled at the top of her lungs as Hannah released another cat.

"It is. You can let her out. I need to grab Gus. One second!"

I blinked as she disappeared out of the store, curly hair flying behind her. Hannah was one of the nicest people I'd ever met. I looked at my feet and for a split second, I thought I was seeing double. Another Ragdoll cat was sitting in front of me, a thoughtful expression on its face. I knelt and held my hand out for inspection. Razzy gave my leg a head bump, nearly knocking me over.

"Careful! My goodness, you can hit hard."

I scratched her behind the ears while her almost twin sniffed my hand. Callie pressed her paws onto my other leg and I went down in a heap, surrounded by inquisitive felines. Well, there are worse things that could happen. I couldn't help but laugh as they swarmed over me. The bell above the door chimed again, and I felt a blast of cold air before it closed.

"Razzy cat! What are you doing to poor Shireen?"

Razzy gave Hannah a slow blink and hopped off my chest. I scrambled to my feet, feeling strangely embarrassed.

"Sorry. They weren't doing anything wrong."

Hannah cocked her head to the side before putting a hand on my arm.

"I'm not mad. I try to teach them good manners but they never listen to me. Alright, Gus, let's get you out so you can join the menagerie. Is Anastasia in the back?"

I nodded as she released an enormous Maine Coon cat from the third carrier. He looked at me and gave me a slow nod before brushing against my leg. These cats were something else.

"Hannah? Shireen? The tea is ready. Come on back."

Hannah looped her arm through mine and led me to the back of the store, chattering a mile a minute. Somehow, she felt like a sister. Well, considering my family, what I assumed a sister would feel like. I relaxed as I lowered myself onto the couch next to the two women. I still wasn't sure why I was here, but it felt good to be included in their group.

"Are you much of a tea drinker, dear?"

I shrugged, uncertain. My mom had made sun tea when I was a kid, but I'd never liked the stuff.

"Not really, but I'll be happy to try some. It smells amazing."

I sniffed the air, trying to place the scents wafting out of the tea pot sitting on the table. It smelled like spring had somehow come early.

"I think you'll enjoy it, but if you don't like it, no worries."

Hannah shot me a smile as Anastasia filled the cups.

"I was never much of a tea drinker either until Anastasia introduced me to it. I think you'll like it. She makes it all herself."

I took a cup and sniffed again before taking a tentative sip. The warm liquid was sweeter than I'd thought it would be.

"Oh, that's good. What's in here?"

Hannah cocked an eyebrow before leaning back so Razzy could climb in her lap.

"I taste the honey, but I'm not sure what the other things are."

I felt whiskers brush my arm and raised it to see the other Ragdoll cat looking at me again. His serious, blue-eyed gaze startled me. I motioned for him to join me and he climbed on my lap, kneading my pants gently, but never taking his eyes off me.

"Does he usually do this?"

"No. He's not bothering you, is he? I trimmed his claws the other day."

I wrapped my free arm around his fuzzy body and shook my head.

"Not at all. It's sweet. You're so lucky to have them. You too, Anastasia. Callie is so sweet."

"She's a doll. You're right on the honey, Hannah. I also put lemon grass in the tea. It's very good for bringing peace in troubled times."

I met Hannah's eyes, unsure of what to say in response. Hannah was well aware of the trouble I'd recently gone through, but I wasn't sure if she'd shared that with Anastasia. I also wasn't sure how I'd feel about it if she had. Hannah shook her head slightly and I let out the breath I'd been holding before taking another sip. Whenever I'm nervous, I have to be doing something with my hands, and right now, if that meant drinking this tea dry, I'd do it. At least it tasted delicious. Hannah seemed to sense my discomfort and put her tea down, smiling at me gently.

"You're probably wondering why I had you meet me here? I've got some news and I think you'll be excited about it."

I wrapped my hands around the mug and leaned forward, intrigued. A few weeks ago, I'd mentioned my dream of becoming a reporter, and Hannah had assured me she'd help.

"Really? What is it?"

"Well, I talked to my old journalism professor, and he mentioned that my university is now doing some online degrees. If you're interested, there's still time to sign up. The nice thing is, it's a study at your own pace program, so you can still work. If you want to, that is."

Hope lanced through me, bright as the sun and I gripped the mug in my hand so hard I thought it might break.

"Seriously? That would be amazing. I don't know how it will work with my job, though. It's pretty demanding."

I work for the estate of a famous actor, Ken Brockman, and my job had me running from early in the morning until late at night. Trying to balance going to school with my schedule was going to be hard. Not impossible, but definitely difficult. The only plus side I could see would be I'd be so busy I wouldn't have time to think about the past. In my situation, that was probably a good thing.

"Well, that's the other part of my news. I know after... well, after what happened," Hannah said, glancing briefly at Anastasia. "Anyway, there's a resort in Valewood, a few hours away, that needs a new public relations person. They offer room and board, just like where you work now. I don't know what you're making now, but the resort's willing to offer you mid five-figures to take the job. Maybe a change of scenery would..."

"I'll do it. When can I start?"

They shared a laugh as Anastasia leaned forward with the teapot. I held out my cup for a refill.

"Trevor, my contact there, said the sooner, the better. It's a nice place. My best friend was married there. It's not perfect, but no place is. The people who work there now are pretty cool. I think you'd fit in."

"I don't have any experience with public relations, though. Don't they want someone who knows what they're doing?"

"I'll be able to help and they offer on-the-job training. Some places like to have people trained the way they want stuff done. Between that, and the courses you'll be taking, you'll catch on quickly."

I took another sip of my tea before glancing down to see Rudy was still staring at me. He blinked slowly, and I stroked his head.

"I'll do it. I'll need to give my two weeks, but this is the most exciting thing that's ever happened to me. I can't believe it."

"While you're up there, maybe there's something you could do for us?" Anastasia asked, chucking Callie under the chin.

"Sure! Anything."

Hannah and Anastasia shared another look before Hannah turned back to me, her face serious.

"There's a clowder of cats there. They live in the woods. That's actually where Callie is from. Would you be able to look in on them and make sure they're fed? I've been worried sick about it being so cold."

"A clowder?"

"It's a group of wild cats who band together. The leader's name is Jasper, but I'm not sure if he's still with us," Hannah said, her voice catching. "If not, Fig will be in charge, I guess."

"You named them? That's so sweet."

Hannah's face blanked, and she blinked several times before nodding.

"Something like that. I'd just be so relieved if I knew they were okay and a fellow cat lover was checking on them."

"Of course. I'd be happy to do that," I said. "I can't believe it. I feel like my whole life just changed in an instant."

Hannah picked Razzy up and gave her a quick squeeze.

"Anything you need, Shireen, just ask. That's what friends are for."

My heart tripped in my chest as I realized I'd never had a friend like Hannah. I didn't know Anastasia yet, but I had a feeling she was cut from the same cloth. I looked down at my hands, feeling the distance between where I was now and where I'd come from.

"If you don't mind, dear, I have a small gift I'd like to give you."

Anastasia rose gracefully and smoothed her long skirt.

"Oh, you don't need to do that."

"I know, but I sense it will be important to you in the months ahead."

She glided out from the back room and I glanced at Hannah, uncertain.

"She does that. Whatever it is, trust me, you'll be glad you have it. I can't tell you how often her gifts have helped me. Anastasia is special."

Rudy chirped at me and I laughed at the earnest expression on his little face.

"Well, if this guy says so, I guess that's enough for me. Look out, Rudy, I need to get up."

He jumped down and was off, chasing Callie like a streak of lightning. Gus and Razzy followed at a more sedate pace while Hannah looped her elbow through mine.

"I'm so glad you're happy about my news. I was a little worried you'd think I was too forward."

"Are you kidding me? This is the nicest thing anyone's ever done for me."

I paused and wrapped Hannah in a hug, surprising us both. She returned the squeeze before patting my back.

"It's all going to work out. I have a feeling you'll be starting a whole new adventure. While you're up there in Valewood, look up Ethan Rhodes. He's a detective on the force up there and a great guy. I think you'll like him."

"Well, hopefully I won't need to contact the police, but I appreciate it."

I didn't say that the last thing I wanted to do was meet another man, but I knew Hannah understood. She'd been the one who'd rescued me from Adam Caldwell, my potentially insane ex-boyfriend. She brushed my hair off my face and nodded.

"Let's see what Anastasia has for you. I'm so excited."

I followed her to the aisle Callie had led me to when I'd first walked in, and we stopped in front of the display of stones. Anastasia was waiting for us, an enigmatic smile on her face. She picked a stone and held it out to me.

I tentatively reached my hand out, and she set the stone there before wrapping my fingers around it.

"Keep this with you. In fact, I've got a corded necklace that will work perfectly. One second."

Hannah winked before following Anastasia to the front of the shop. I carefully opened my fingers and looked at the rock. It was smooth and warm to the touch. I ran my thumb over it and felt something deep within my heart stir. Startled, I closed my hand in a fist, noticing that all four cats were staring at me expectantly. Rudy meowed, and they continued watching me.

"Um, hi, guys. Is everything okay?"

Rudy let out what sounded remarkably like an "erf" of frustration and closed his beautiful blue eyes.

I shook my head before rejoining Hannah and Anastasia. I handed over the stone while she strung it onto a cord.

"Thank you so much, but please, let me pay for it. At least for the cord."

Anastasia shook her head and came closer, draping the cord over my neck. My hand instinctively went up to the stone, and I closed my fist around it again.

"I appreciate the offer, but this is a gift, freely given. May you find it useful."

I wasn't sure what to think, but the woman's kindness warmed me to my core. I tucked the stone inside my shirt.

"I'll text you all the information you'll need to contact the resort and accept their offer. I'll send the link to the enrollment page for the university, too. My professor said he'd keep an eye out for your application and prioritize it."

Tears swam through my eyes at the kindness flowing around me. I was too overwhelmed to speak and settled for hugging each of them. I dropped to my knees and did the same with each cat before standing again.

"Well, here's to starting fresh! Hannah, I can't thank you enough."

"Anytime you need anything, I'm just a call away. Anastasia, too."

I couldn't imagine needing anything from the ethereal shop owner, but I appreciated the sentiment. I nodded at both of them before heading to the door, feet buoyed with excitement. I waved one more time and walked outside. Right before the door closed, a small voice piped up. I didn't recognize it, but I just caught the words before the door swung shut.

"Please say hello to Ollie for me."

I cocked my head to the side, startled. Who was that? It sounded like it was coming from the store, but it wasn't Hannah or Anastasia's voice. I shook off the feeling and headed back to my car. When I'd left the estate that morning, I'd been excited for something new to do on my day off, but I didn't know it would be so life changing. I got back in and fired up the little engine, saying a quick prayer it would get me back to the house. I had a lot of planning to do.

# Chapter Two

I stared up at the facade of the Brockman house before looking at the small crowd who'd gathered to see me off. I'd lived and worked with these people for so long, they'd become my adopted family. Marcie, the cook, bustled forward, carrying a cloth bag.

"This is for you, sweetheart. It's just a couple of snacks for the road. You know how expensive and terrible gas station food is. This should tide you over."

She wrapped her massive arms around me and squeezed me so tight I'm pretty sure I almost saw stars.

"Thanks, Marcie. You're the best. I can't wait to dig in."

She clucked her tongue as she used her thumb to wipe away a tear that had somehow escaped my eyes.

"Don't cry, love. You're going to do great things. Don't forget about us once you're at that fancy resort."

"I wouldn't dream of it. Thank you, Marcie. For everything."

She squeezed me again and turned away, but not before I saw a few tears streaking down her cheeks. When I'd accepted the job offer, I didn't know how hard it was going to be to leave this estate, even with everything that happened here. I smiled as Tiffany scuffed her foot on the pavement.

"Gonna miss you, Shir."

"I'm going to miss you, too, Tiffany. Thanks for always being there for me."

She grabbed me for a quick hug before glancing over her shoulder.

"We'd better make it quick, guys. You know how Nathan is. He won't appreciate us standing around. I don't want to get written up again. Later, Shir."

I nodded and looked back at my car. Dave, the chauffeur, had given me a free oil change, but he'd instructed me to take it slow. Luckily, that was all my car knew how to do.

"Did I miss her?"

I spun around to see Raylynn at the top of the steps. Even though Nathan called the shots at the Brockman estate, she was the person I reported to as a member of the housekeeping staff.

"I'm still here."

Raylynn smoothed her hair as she jogged down the steps.

"Here. Before you go, we all chipped in on a little something for you."

I took the bag she was holding and gasped. No way. I opened the zipper a little and peeked inside, confirming it held a laptop.

"You shouldn't have. My goodness! No way."

"Hey, you're going to need it for your studies. I'm proud of you, Shireen. Tell Hannah hi for me if you talk to her."

I wrapped my arms around the laptop bag, hugging it to my chest as I nodded. Even though Hannah and her lovable menagerie had only stayed for a weekend, they'd imprinted themselves on all our hearts.

"I will. Thank you, Raylynn. You've been the best boss. I'm sorry to go."

"I'll miss you, but you're on to better and brighter things. Chin up, girl. Go out there and show 'em what you've got."

She gave me an awkward one-armed hug before scuttling back up the stairs. I waved at everyone before opening the door to my car and stowing the laptop in the backseat. Marcie's bag was going in the front with me. There was no way I was missing out on her treats.

A pang of sadness hit me as I got buckled in and looked at the house one last time. The odds of me returning were small, but I hoped I'd never lose touch with the people who guided me through one of the hardest periods of my life to date. I gave a cheery wave and put the car in drive, resisting the urge to look over my shoulder once I was on my way.

I clicked the link to the directions Hannah sent and took a steadying breath. I was doing it. I was actually doing it. Joy replaced the bittersweet feeling in my chest as I drove down the long, winding driveway to the main road.

The bag of treats in the passenger seat beckoned, but I forced myself to wait until I was on the interstate before giving into the temptation. No one cooked like Marcie, and from the smells coming from the bag, she'd included a few of my favorite cinnamon rolls in there.

I turned up the radio and bobbed my head along to an unfamiliar song as I replayed the past two weeks in my head. From accepting the job offer to getting signed up for the journalism program, it had been a blur. I shook my head as I focused on the road. Just three more hours and I'd be at the place where I'd launch the next phase of my life.

Traffic picked up as I neared Golden Hills, and before I knew it, I was following the instructions to exit the interstate and get onto the highway for the resort. I stopped to get gas and rummaged through my bag of treats, smiling as I confirmed what my nose already knew. Cinnamon roll.

I happily scarfed it down and hit the road again, looking around the trees as I drove. From what I could tell, I was steadily climbing. I'd done a little research on the resort where I'd be working, but the pictures certainly hadn't done the area justice. The snow-swept vistas called to me, begging to be explored. Hopefully, I'd find time to get some hiking in. I glanced down at my phone, confirming I had about forty-five minutes of driving left.

The sun dropped behind the mountains in front of me and I cranked up my heater. My car made a terrible banging noise under the hood, and I gripped the steering wheel tighter.

"No. Just a little further. You can do it."

It chugged for a few seconds before evening out and I let out a breath. Somehow, my encouragement paid off. I was no mechanic, and I was clueless about what that sound was, but as long as I was moving, everything would be okay. Right?

I turned off the radio and rolled my neck, dislodging my braid from its spot on my shoulder. The light faded fast, and I clicked on my high beams as I slowed down. The last thing I wanted to do was run smack into a deer. The banging noise came back and my heart tripped.

"Come on, girl. Just a little further."

This time, my encouragement fell on deaf ears. The chugging started again before my dash went black and the car engine cut off. Panic lanced through my chest as I steered towards the shoulder and slapped on my hazards.

"You've gotta be kidding me."

I put my head on the steering wheel and turned the key. I just needed a few more miles. Nothing.

"Okay, Shireen. Think."

I groped for my phone in the dark and hit the button. No service. My heart beat faster as I looked up and down the road. There'd been nothing back the way I'd come, and I didn't know what was ahead. Well, I knew there were a bunch of trees. They crowded along the road on both sides. I'd found them beautiful, but now I was terrified of what might hide within them. Were there bears in this part of Colorado?

"Lions and tigers and bears, oh my."

I needed to figure this out, and fast. I pulled the zipper up on my coat to block out the chill filling the car. I snagged the beanie I'd discarded earlier and pulled it down over my ears.

Suddenly, bright lights hit my windshield, blinding me. I held up a hand to block them out before realizing I should ask for help. A different terror gripped me around the middle.

I threw open the door and jumped out, waving my arms around like a madwoman. The truck cruised to a stop, and the window rolled down.

"You need help, miss?"

The man's face was covered with a beard, but I could see his kind eyes. I tamped down the fear coursing through me and nodded.

"Yes, please. My car just died. I'm on my way to the Valewood resort. Do you know how far away it is?"

The man turned off the truck's engine and opened the door. As he stepped out, I kept craning my neck until I could see his eyes. Holy smokes. Between his height, the thick beard and the puffy black coat he was wearing, if I didn't know better, I'd swear I was talking to a bear.

"It's just up the road. I'm Trevor, I work there."

"Trevor from security?"

He nodded and cocked his head to the side.

"Do I know you?"

"I'm Shireen. We talked on the phone."

His bear-like face creased into a smile as he put his hands on his hips.

"Well, I call this a happy accident. Let me look at your car and see if we can get you back on the road. It's nice to put a face to the name."

I trotted after him and hopped in to pop the hood on my car before joining him.

"What are the odds?" I asked, peering into the engine. "I can't believe I ran into you."

"How's Hannah?"

I smiled as the common thread that seemed to direct my life came up.

"She's great. I'm supposed to call her as soon as I arrive. What do you think is wrong with it?"

Trevor shot me a grin as he closed the hood.

"Well, at first glance, I'd say it's broken, but I'm not a mechanic. Tell you what. Let's get your things into my truck and I'll take you to the resort. We'll sort this out in the morning. It's getting late and you look cold."

I shook my head as I twisted my hands together.

"I don't want to be a bother. I don't have service on my phone. Maybe you could call me a tow truck and I'll take it from there?"

"Not a chance. This time of the night, they'll charge you a fortune. It's not that far, and I'd rather see you there safely."

I tried to protest, but he lumbered past me and began grabbing my bags from the backseat. I snagged my purse and the rest of Marcie's treats before following him back to the pickup.

"Are you sure? I hate to keep you from whatever you were doing?"

"I'm positive, and I was just going home. Annie, that's my wife, won't mind. I'll call her on the way back and let her know I'll be late."

He tossed my bags in the backseat of his enormous truck and gave me a hand to clamber up. I put my hands in my lap as he walked around and got in.

"Let's just get turned around and we'll be there in a jiffy."

I glanced back at my poor car as we pulled away. It had done its best. I didn't want to think about the cost to get it fixed and focused instead on Trevor.

"Have you worked at Valewood for a long time?"

"Quite a few years now. It's a nice place. We've had our share of troubles, but we're a solid team now. I think you'll like it there. Did Hannah tell you about what happened?"

"The murder? Yes. What a horrible thing."

"Yeah, we all miss Billy. We've gone through a few changes, but everyone is moving past it as best we can."

I nodded and looked out the window as the sea of trees opened up. The moon was already high in the sky, casting its silver glow on the surrounding mountains. My breath caught in my chest as we came around a corner and the resort came into view.

"Shireen. That's an interesting name," Trevor said.

"It's what my mom picked," I said, making a face. "Trust me, it wasn't my choice. I'd change it if I could."

"Why don't you?"

I shrugged and looked back out the window.

"I don't know. I never really thought about the mechanics of it."

"You could do what I do and just use your middle name. It's all perfectly legal then. No paperwork."

"Trevor's your middle name? What's your first name?"

"Gerald," he said, making a face just like the one I'd made. "Never could stand it. I don't know what my parents were thinking. I've been Trevor since I was a little kid. What's your middle name?"

"Eden."

"I like it. It fits you."

I mouthed the name to myself as a little bubble of joy worked its way through my chest.

"You know what? I like it, too. I'm starting fresh and why not do it with a fresh name? Eden it is."

Trevor grinned at me, his white teeth flashing in his beard.

"That'll be five bucks," he said, winking. "Here we are. I'll walk you in and take you to the front desk so you can get your key."

"You don't need to go to all this extra trouble, Trevor."

"Psshh. A whole fifteen minutes out of my day. What will I do?"

As I got out of the truck, I smiled to myself. So far, my first encounter with a coworker had gone swimmingly. If the rest of the people here were like Trevor, this place might just be perfect. I grabbed my purse as he got the rest of my bags and headed for the front door of the lodge. I turned in a slow circle, admiring what I could see of the resort in the night. I couldn't wait to see it by day.

"Are you coming, Eden?"

I looked up at the sound of my new name and nodded, scurrying up the steps after him. This place was turning out to be alright.

# Chapter Three

My jaw dropped as I followed Trevor up to the front desk of the lodge. The pictures I'd seen online were completely lacking in replicating the sheer grandiosity of the space. Even though I'd worked at an estate owned by a famous movie star, this place took my breath away. I tore my eyes away from the massive beams on the ceiling and made eye contact with the girl behind the counter.

Her freckled face was lit with a cheery smile as she leaned over to shake my head.

"Hiya. I'm Charlie. Trevor said you're here to report for duty?"

She gave me a sassy salute as she cracked her gum.

"Yep. I'm Shir... Eden Brooks."

Charlie made a face and cocked her head to the side.

"That's an interesting name."

Trevor laughed and shook his head.

"She suffers from the same thing I have, hatemyfirstnameitis. The paperwork says Shireen, but she's going by Eden."

"What is your first name, anyway?" Charlie asked as she shuffled through the papers on the desk. "And I love the name Eden. It suits you. Especially with all that gorgeous hair."

I fingered the braid on my shoulder and shrugged. Growing up, I'd never been allowed to cut it, other than to trim the split ends. Even after I'd left home and gone out into the world, I still hadn't cut it. Most days it went into a tight braid. Maybe it was time for a change. I shook off my thoughts and smiled at Charlie.

"Thanks. I like your hair, too."

She leaned forward and whispered across the desk.

"Check this out."

She flipped up the underside of her shoulder length dark brown hair, revealing a bright cherry red color.

"Oh! I'd never know you have it dyed. That's beautiful."

She winked before typing on the computer.

"Looks like you've got Cabin Ten. Sweet! We'll be neighbors. Or almost neighbors. I'm eight. We'll have to hang out sometime. I can show you the ropes."

Trevor levered himself off the desk and put his hands on his hips.

"Before I forget, Charlie, can you leave a note for the morning crew to call the tow company? Her car is right by mile marker thirty-four. It can go to the garage in Valewood."

"Bummer," Charlie said, frowning as she wrote on a sticky note. "The garage guys are good, though. Not too expensive."

"I hope not. Until I get it fixed, I'm stranded here."

"No worries," Trevor said. "One of us can take you into town if you need to go. I'll walk you over to your cabin and give you a quick tour on the way. The rest can wait until daylight. Not much to see in the dark, anyway.

"I hate to keep you when I'm sure you need to get home. You've already done so much."

"Don't worry about it. I'm happy to help. Besides, this one here will talk your ear off and I don't want you to run screaming into the woods," he said, thumbing in Charlie's direction.

"Speaking of the woods, Hannah mentioned there were some cats in the area?"

Charlie nodded and cracked her gum again.

"There are a few. With the snow, I haven't seen them as often, though."

My heart sank as I realized finding the clowder wouldn't be easy in the dead of winter. I'd promised Hannah to look after them, and I couldn't imagine letting her down.

"They're definitely around. Luke leaves out food every night, and he says it's always gone by the next time he's out there. Do you like cats, Eden?" Trevor asked.

"I love them. Hopefully, I'll be able to see them."

Charlie slid a card across the desk towards me and I slid it into my pocket.

"Here you go. If you need anything, just ring the desk from the phone in your room. I'm here until six most days."

"Wow, that's a long shift."

She pulled a book out from under the counter and winked at me again.

"Gives me time to read. Whoops, I probably shouldn't have said that in front of the security guy," she said in a stage whisper behind her hand.

"Yeah, yeah. Like we can't see the desk from our cameras," Trevor said, rolling his eyes good-naturedly. "Let's get you settled."

I waved to Charlie and followed Trevor's bear-like form back outside. The wind whipped through the vestibule, and I wrapped my coat tighter around my body. If this was the usual temperature, I'd need to upgrade my wardrobe.

"The cabins for the staff are all back here," Trevor said, pointing ahead. "Each one has a ductless unit that you can set to whatever temp you want. They work pretty well, or they did when I lived here."

"You've worked here a long time?" I asked, jogging through the snow to keep up.

"I have. It's a good place. We've got some fresh faces, but everyone gets along really well. Do you see that building right over there?"

I followed the direction he was pointing and nodded.

"That's the dining hall. Breakfast starts at seven. The rest of the meals are at the usual times, unless we've got a big event going on," he said, looking at his watch. "You missed dinner, though. Do you need any food?"

"No, I've got plenty of snacks left. They'll tide me over till morning."

"You'll be working in the lodge. James will be here in the morning and he'll get you all set up."

I tamped down the butterflies circling in my stomach and came to a stop in front of my cabin. Here it was. My home for the foreseeable future. I couldn't see much of it in the dark, but it was bigger than I expected.

"Thanks, Trevor. For everything," I said, swiping the card in the reader.

"The remote for the heating unit's right by the door. Don't be afraid to call Charlie if you need anything. See you tomorrow!" Trevor said, giving me a thumbs up before heading back the way we came.

The door swung open, and I stepped in, closing the door behind me. Plunged into darkness, I groped around for the light switch and held my breath as I clicked it on. Once my eyes adjusted, I couldn't believe the space. I spun around in a slow circle, taking it all in.

The main room held a bed, a desk, a small kitchenette, and, from the looks of it, a bathroom off to the side. It was small, but the little decor touches made it feel homey. I set my bags down and turned around, looking for the remote Trevor mentioned.

"There you are," I said, jumping a little as my voice echoed through the space.

I hit the power button and set the temperature. Warm air immediately flowed out from the unit hanging above the door and I stood there for a second, soaking it in. Once the room warmed, I shrugged out of my jacket and hung it up on the hook by the door.

I flopped onto the bed and bounced a little. Not bad. I could get used to this. I sat cross-legged and nodded. Time to unpack.

Once I'd stowed away my clothes, I set my laptop up on the desk and smiled at it. My first brand new laptop. Joy filled my heart as I powered it on. I still couldn't believe the crew surprised me with it. Once I got through the set up, I pulled open the notes application and stared at the screen for a few seconds before typing a to-do list.

"First, get the car fixed. Ugh," I said, playing with my braid. "That's not gonna be cheap."

Worry flitted around my head. I'd saved a nice nest egg, but it wouldn't last long if things like this kept happening. Thank goodness I'd taken this job. I wasn't sure how or when I'd get paid, but it was certainly going to come in handy.

I jotted down a few more things and closed the laptop, looking around the room again. A small television was hung in the corner, but I didn't feel like watching anything. All I wanted to do was finish the food Marcie had packed and go to bed. I stood and stretched away the kinks from driving and walked over to the kitchenette to rummage through the bag.

"Sweet! A PB & J," I said to myself, pulling the sandwich out.

Marcie knew my weakness, and her thoughtfulness made tears threaten again. Geez, today was turning me into a watering pot. I unwrapped my sandwich and took a bite, closing my eyes as the flavor of Marcie's homemade strawberry jam smacked me in the mouth. I was going to miss that woman's food.

I was halfway through the first triangle when I heard voices outside my window. I stopped chewing and leaned closer to hear. The other cabins had been dark when I approached. Maybe it was another co-worker coming home. I shook my head and pulled back when I heard what sounded like a woman's voice.

"Looks like someone new moved into this cabin. Her smell is unique."

My stomach knotted immediately. What the heck? I leaned closer to the window, all thoughts of eavesdropping being wrong evaporating.

"I wonder what she's like. Do you think she'll be like the one lady?"

The second voice was lower and sounded male. I crept towards the door as questions crowded around in my head. What did they mean by my smell? I showered regularly. I surreptitiously got in a pit sniff as I leaned closer to the door. As far as I could tell, I smelled fine.

"I doubt it. Jasper said he's only known one other person like her. Let's go."

Where had I heard that name before? I heard the snow under my window crunch and fear reared up. Who was standing out there talking about me? I threw open the door and looked out into the darkness. No one was around. Strange. A scurrying sound pulled my head to the left, and I squinted as two slight forms shot through the snow, kicking up little puffs. Were those cats?

They disappeared from sight as a gust of wind blew snow in my face. I sputtered and leaned back into my cabin, closing the door. I rubbed my hands together and moved towards the kitchen. My appetite had fled, but I didn't want to waste my sandwich. I wrapped up the remaining half and stuck it in the fridge while I thought.

Should I call Charlie? I didn't see anyone out there, but I definitely heard voices. Would she think I was nuts? Most likely. Right now, replaying it in my head, it seemed a little nuts. Maybe the long day had gotten to me.

I shook my head and flipped on the television, desperate for a distraction. We'd never been allowed to watch television growing up, and it was still a novelty to me. I got into my pajamas and got into bed, pulling the blankets up to underneath my chin. Maybe I had imagined it. But why had I seen cats running away? I tried to focus on the news, but quickly lost interest.

The noise of the television droned in the background as my eyes got heavy. Whatever it had been, it was going to wait until tomorrow. I snuggled into the comfortable mattress and clicked the off button on the remote. Maybe sleep was just what I needed.

# Chapter Four

I stood outside the dining hall, hesitating. What would the other employees be like? So far, Trevor and Charlie were incredible, but was everyone going to be as nice? Anxiety gripped me and I fiddled with my braid as I paced back and forth.

"Eden! There you are. I was wondering if you slept in," Charlie said, rounding the corner. "What are we waiting for?"

Her hair was up in a ponytail and her freckled nose was wrinkled against the cold as she stared at the door.

"Um, I'm not sure. I just go in and get breakfast?"

She tucked her arm into mine and pulled me ahead.

"Yep. Easy peasy. Just follow my lead. I'll introduce you to everyone."

She bounced ahead, ponytail flying. I had no choice but to follow, but I pulled up short once I entered. This place was enormous! The soaring ceiling with exposed beams caught my attention, followed shortly by the long buffet table stretching out in front of us.

"Wow! All this food is for us?"

"Take your pic. There's a waffle station and an omelet bar, or you can just pick from what's already prepared. Ooo, they have my favorite hash browns! Let's go before they're all scooped up. Danny always tries to beat me to the punch."

She pushed a plate into my hand and walked ahead, heading straight for the potatoes. The selection was almost overwhelming and everything smelled heavenly. I'd been worried about missing Marcie's food, but this was on a whole other level.

"Eden, over here! You gotta try these. I saved you a few."

Charlie grinned as she shoveled a heaping pile onto my plate. The spoon rattled as she tossed it back into the now-empty tray. I looked back and forth and tried to figure out my next move. Eggs. Scrambled eggs always hit the spot. I scooped those up and added some crispy bacon before walking to the end of the buffet to grab my utensils.

Charlie was joking with an older woman while she waited for me.

"Iris, this is Eden. She's our new PR guru."

I juggled my tray and reached out a hand to Wendy.

"I don't know about guru, but I'm ready to learn. What do you do here?"

"I'm on the kitchen staff. We used to be a catering only place, but after last summer, management created the resort's own in-house kitchen. I love it here."

Her friendly face was creased in a smile as she shook my hand before glancing at the empty hash brown tray.

"I'd better remove that tray. I should've known you'd snag the rest."

"Lemme know if there's anymore in the back," Charlie said, giving Iris a cheeky grin.

Iris playfully swatted her shoulder and rolled her eyes.

"That's it and you know it. You're lucky you got some. I saw Danny eyeing the tray a few minutes ago."

"My day is made. Come on, Eden, let's grab a table."

I followed the bubbly Charlie as she plopped down at a table with only two seats left. I took a deep breath before carefully placing my tray on the table and perching on the end of my seat.

"Danny, of the voracious appetite, Carl, Denise, and Wendy, this is Eden. She's our new PR person."

She pointed out each person, and I struggled to assign their names in my head as I smiled at each one.

"Hi Eden," Danny said, leaning over with his fork at the ready to snag some hash browns off of Charlie's plate. "Nice to meet you. I'm the valet, slash bellhop, slash doorman."

"Watch it, buster," Charlie said, waving her fork threateningly before moving her arm in front of her plate. "You know as well as I do we only get these once a week. I'm not giving you a shred."

Danny eyed my plate before shrugging.

"Oh well. There's always next week. Where are you from Eden?"

"Danny, let her eat," Wendy said, her voice warm. "You can talk after you've eaten, honey."

I bobbed my head before taking my first bite of the potatoes. Wow, Charlie wasn't kidding. These were seriously good. My stomach kicked into gear as I sampled the eggs.

"Oh, Wendy, did you call a tow for Eden's car?" Charlie asked as she scraped her plate.

"I did. I'm so sorry that happened to you. Lucky for you, Trevor was heading home. He was the last off-site employee to leave. It would've been a long, cold walk. Anyway, they picked it up this morning and they'll call us when they figure out what's wrong with it. I gave them the resort phone since I didn't know your number."

I swallowed some bacon and nodded.

"Thank you. I appreciate it. Do all of you live here?"

Everyone nodded and started talking at once.

"One at a time," Charlie said, heaving a deep sigh as she finished her potatoes. "Let's not overwhelm poor Eden. Carl, you go first. Name, rank, and serial number."

Carl rolled his eyes and flashed a quick smile in my direction, his warm brown eyes kind. He ran a hand over his thinning hair.

"I'm the new groundskeeper. Right now, I'm mostly shoveling snow, but in spring, we have a plan to redo the gardens. I'm in cabin five."

Denise looked around and shrugged, her sharp blond bob swinging over her shoulders.

"I guess I'll go next. I'm Denise, cabin four. I'm in HR and it's my job to keep these yahoos in line. Speaking of which, when you have time later today, stop by my office and I'll get your paperwork updated."

I appreciated her not mentioning my name change in front of everyone and shot Charlie a grateful smile that she'd smoothed things over for me.

"Thanks, Denise. I'll do that."

Wendy straightened and flashed me a friendly smile.

"I'm Wendy. Cabin one. I like long hikes in the forest and paddling around the lake..."

Everyone at the table groaned in unison, but Wendy powered through.

"And I'm the day desk manager," she said, sticking her tongue out at everyone. "It's nice to meet you, Eden."

"Your turn, Eden," Charlie said, leaning over the table and grabbing the remains of the roll on his plate.

"Hey! I was gonna eat that."

"You snooze, you lose."

I cleared my throat and grabbed a glass of water from the table, suddenly feeling self-conscious. Everyone was so nice, but I couldn't help feeling like I was under a microscope.

"I'm Eden Brooks. I used to work at the Brockman estate. Right now, I'm taking some journalism classes and, as you know, I'll be working in PR."

"No way!" Charlie said, turning towards me. "Do you mean like Ken Brockman?"

"That's the one. I worked at his house down by Golden Hills."

"Oh man, that is so cool," Danny said, leaning closer. "What's he like? I love that show he's in. Is he really a cowboy?"

I bit my lip as I weighed my answer. I didn't want to be the one to burst anyone's bubble, but my experiences with the actor hadn't been the greatest.

"He only came to the estate a few times a year, so I didn't see him much. I worked in housekeeping."

"He's so handsome," Denise said, holding her hand up to her heart. "I can't imagine being in the same house with him. You're so lucky,"

"Well, if she was that lucky, she wouldn't be here," Charlie said, popping a fresh piece of gum into her mouth. "There's a story there, but we'll wait until you're ready to tell it."

She winked at me and leaned back in her chair, glancing towards the giant clock on the wall.

"It's about that time, isn't it?" Danny said, groaning as he moved his chair back. "Back to the grind. Nice meeting you, Eden. Lunch is a bit of a grab-and-go situation, but join us for dinner."

"I'm gonna go back to bed and grab a few more hours of sleep," Charlie said, stretching as she stood. "I'll come by and we'll grab lunch together."

My insides were full of warm fuzzies as I grabbed my plate and smiled at everyone at the table. This place had a real family feel and I could already tell I was going to like these people. I thought about the cats I'd seen the night before and hurried to catch up to Charlie.

"Hey, Charlie. I think I saw a few of those cats last night. Trevor mentioned Luke is the one who feeds them?"

Charlie stacked her plate and pointed towards a tall, thin man standing behind the buffet table.

"That's him. He's super shy, but really nice. I'll introduce you."

I trailed behind her as she waved at Luke.

"Hey, Luke. Gotta another cat lover here. This is Eden."

Luke's bony face was graced with a set of remarkable hazel eyes that lit from within as he looked at me.

"Nice to meet you, Eden."

"If you ever want any help with the cats, I'd love to lend a hand. I promised a friend I'd check on them."

He nodded, his Adam's apple bobbing in his throat.

"Sure. I usually go after dinner. I'd love some help."

I grinned and turned to follow Charlie back into the cold,

buoyed by how easily things were going. Then, remembering I'd yet to meet my boss, my anxiety came rushing back.

"See you later, Eden. Meet you for lunch a little after noon? I'll introduce you to everyone else then."

She waved and shoved her hands into her pockets, kicking up snow as she walked back to the cabins. I turned and looked at the lodge. No time like the present. I took a few steps and heard my name.

"Hang on, I'll walk with you," Wendy said, gasping a little as she hustled through the snow.

"Thanks. I'm not sure where I need to meet Mr. Marsburg."

"All the offices are in the back. I'll show you where to go," she said, holding the door open for me.

The warmth of the lobby rushed over me and I held my face up to the heater. Another woman was behind the desk, but she didn't smile as we approached.

"Took you long enough. It's a good thing I ate earlier."

"Sorry, Penny. Eden's new and we got carried away," Wendy said, her cheeks flushing. "You can get back to what you were doing."

Penny sniffed loudly before standing. She gave me the once over and dismissed me before smoothing her already immaculate pantsuit. Her black hair was scraped back into what looked like the tightest bun I'd ever seen. She stalked off, heels clicking on the polished wood floor.

Wendy leaned closer.

"That's Penny. She's in charge of the housekeeping staff. Don't mind her, she's always that way. I think her mother knew it when she named her. She always turns up at the wrong time."

"Hey, it's okay. Besides, if everyone was friendly, I'd think I'd stumbled into a horror movie," I said, laughing off Penny's unfriendliness.

"I like the way you think. Just head on back through those doors. Mr. Marsburg's office is the first door on the right. I'll let you know if I hear anything from the garage about your car."

I nodded and took a deep breath before heading through the

French doors she'd pointed to. The long hallway stretched in front of me and I stopped in front of the door with my boss' name on it. I rapped once and waited.

"Come on in."

Well, he sounded friendly. I opened the door and stepped in, nearly gasping as I saw the floor to ceiling window behind the desk. The man at the desk smiled as he followed my eyes.

"It's a beautiful view, isn't it? My father designed this office, and it's one of the best things about working here. Have a seat, Shireen, or sorry, Eden. I'm James."

He stuck his hand across the desk and I shook it.

"It's nice to meet you. I hope the name change idea is okay."

He leaned back in his chair, his chestnut hair gleaming under the sunlight streaming in.

"Not a problem at all. I know all about fresh starts. I wanted to be a chef and look at me now," he said, chuckling. "You came highly recommended, Miss Brooks. The position you're filling is new, but I have no doubts you'll do a great job."

I swallowed hard, wishing I felt the same way.

"I'll do the best I can. I've reviewed the job description and I've been studying in my spare time. I've got a few ideas for some promotional materials."

"No rush. Get settled in and we'll talk next week. I don't expect you to sprint right out of the gate," he said, waving an elegant hand. "Let's go see your office."

He jumped up, his trim figure blocking the sun for a second as he walked around the desk. He was wearing a pressed shirt with an open collar and a pair of navy blue slacks, tailored impeccably.

I stood and walked through the door he held open. He turned to the right and opened the door two down from him. He flipped on the light and I walked in, surprised at the size of the office.

"Wow, this is very nice."

"It's a little small," he said, handsome face crinkling. "But you have a window at least. Let's get some light in here."

He opened the blinds and nodded.

I moved behind the desk and put my hand on the chair. I was

doing it. I was starting a new career. I'd come a long way from being in housekeeping and although I still wasn't confident, I could only hope it would come with time.

"Thank you, Mr. Marsburg. I'll get settled in. I've already got a plan to get certified in public relations through an online course."

He flashed a set of blinding white teeth.

"Perfect. If you need anything, you know where I am. Sorry to hear about your car. If you need an advance on your salary, just let me know."

I nodded, unsure of how to respond. Tears pricked my eyelids as I struggled to keep it together. He looked at me for a second and nodded again before turning to leave. He shut the door behind him and I sank down into my new office chair. Was all this space really mine?

I spun my chair in a circle and shook my head in disbelief. It had been a warm welcome, minus Penny. I had room and board, and the chance to make something of myself. I had a feeling this was the start of something truly special.

## Chapter Five

B efore I knew it, the window letting light into my office had gone dark and I was squinting to see my computer screen. I powered it down and stood, stretching out the kinks in my back. I'd worked through lunch and my stomach let me know it didn't appreciate it. I took one more look around my office before stepping into the hallway and closing the door. I still couldn't believe it was mine.

The other offices were quiet as I made my way towards the front desk. I'd have to visit Denise tomorrow. Wendy was busy checking a couple in, and from the looks of it, they weren't happy. I slowed my steps and paused behind a luckily placed pillar.

"We were told we would have the suite. We're here for our anniversary," the man said, his face dark.

"I'm so sorry, sir," Wendy said, tapping away on the computer. "But we don't have any suites available. Do you remember who you talked with?"

"She said her name was Penny. She was rude. I remember that."

"Honey, it's okay. A regular room will be just fine," his wife said, tugging on his arm, blue eyes pleading. "Don't worry about it."

High heels clacked on the polished floor, and I swiveled my head to see Penny stalking towards the desk.

"What's going on here?"

Wendy's face was flushed as she turned to Penny.

"This couple says you promised them a suite, but they were registered for a regular room."

Penny leaned over the desk, her shoulder bumping the man. His eyes narrowed and red began creeping up his neck.

"I remember. I specifically told you there were no suites available. Don't pull a fast one on Wendy here and throw me under the buss," Penny said. "Wendy may not be the sharpest tool in the shed, but what's on the computer is what you paid for."

"I would like to speak to the manager," the man said, his voice rising.

"Honey, no, it's okay."

Penny's lips quirked into a cruel smile.

"I'm the highest ranking member on the staff right now. If you have a problem, you'll have to take it up with me."

The wife heaved a sigh and turned to Wendy.

"Could we please have our room key? The regular is fine. We've been driving for hours and I just want to get some sleep."

Wendy nodded and grabbed two keys, pushing them through what I assumed was the programmer. The husband got closer to Penny and shoved his finger into her chest. My heart sped up, and I gripped my bag tighter.

"I will not forget this. You're going to wish you never messed with me."

Penny smoothed her hair and laughed before turning on her heel. The man fisted his hands at his side while his wife grabbed the keys and tugged on his arm.

"Come on, honey. It will be fine. Let's go sleep and everything will be okay tomorrow."

He continued glaring in the direction Penny walked and a chill went down my spine. I'd seen that look in someone's eyes before and hoped I'd never see it again. My hand cramped, and I took a slow breath, releasing the hold on my bag.

I waited until they were out of sight before tiptoeing over to the desk.

"Are you okay, Wendy?"

Her cheeks were stained red as she angrily stacked some folders on the desk.

"I'm fine. It's not the first time that's happened. If you ask me, Penny has a thing about couples. It's like she takes great joy in ruining their vacations. I'm going to talk to Mr. Marsburg about this. I hate to be a narc, but we're going to get a bad name if this keeps happening."

"What do you mean, couples? She's done this before?"

Wendy scratched the side of her nose as she nodded.

"Last time it was a young couple spending their honeymoon here. They swore they had a reservation, but there was nothing on the computer. I felt terrible, but Mr. Marsburg made it all work out. Luckily, he knew someone staying here that weekend and offered to comp their stay if they agreed to transfer to one of the employee cabins."

"If Penny runs housekeeping, why is she working the front desk?"

Wendy let out a breath, sending her bangs skyward.

"We're short staffed. Right now, it's just Charlie and me, and we can't be at the desk all the time."

"Why don't you guys train me and I can help?" I asked. "I'm a quick study."

A smile crept across Wendy's face and she nodded.

"You know what? That might work. Let's ask the boss tomorrow. I think once we tell him what happened tonight, he'll be more apt to agree. I know his family's known Penny for ages, but this has to stop. Great idea, Eden."

I patted her arm.

"How much longer do you have on your shift? If you're hungry, I can watch the desk."

She waved me off.

"No, you've been slaving in your office all day. Charlie will be here in an hour and I packed a dinner tonight," she said, patting her tummy. "I can't keep eating at the buffet every night."

"I think you look great," I said. "See you tomorrow?"

"You got it. Thanks, Eden. I appreciate your help. You're going to fit in here just great."

I dipped my head and shrugged before slinging my bag over my shoulder.

She gave me a cheery wave as I headed outside. I shuffled through the snow to my cabin, pulling my coat closer to my body.

"Hey, Eden!"

I turned and peered through the gloom before spotting Danny as he popped out of his cabin.

"Hi, Danny."

"There she is. We missed you at lunch."

"Sorry, I got tied up in the courses I'm taking for my job. I've got a few days before my college courses kick in and I want to make sure I learn everything I can, so I'm not trying to cram too much into my poor brain at once."

"You must be starving," he said, falling in beside me. "I can't imagine missing a meal. Learn anything good?"

"A few things. It's a blur, but I think it will come together."

I crossed my gloved fingers. I'd hoped I'd be a quick study, but it felt like turning on a garden hose right to the face.

"You'll do great. I can tell. Ready to get some dinner?"

My stomach lurched and let out an angry growl that made Danny laugh.

"Yeah. Will it be buffet style like breakfast? That was pretty cool."

"Yep. We usually get a choice of at least two meats or a veggie option, and then the sides. That's what I'm here for."

"Let me guess... mashed potatoes?"

He made a shocked face and clapped a hand to his chest.

"How did you guess?"

I laughed as I followed him into the dining hall. He really was a character. I spotted Charlie waving like a madwoman before she jogged in our direction.

"Hey, Eden. How was the first day?"

"Good. My brain feels broken, but it was good."

"Isn't James dreamy?"

She batted her eyelashes before making a face at Danny as he groaned.

"Oh no. I don't think I can sit through another conversation on the wonder that is Mr. Marsburg. You'll turn my stomach. Aha! That's your plan, isn't it, Charlie?" Danny asked, tapping the side of his head. "You think you'll get more potatoes than I do? I'm on to you."

The gleam in her eyes gave Danny's question more weight before she cackled.

"Busted. He is hot, though."

"I guess," I said, grabbing a plate. "What's the best thing to have for dinner here?"

"Ooo, try the chicken," Danny said, making a chef's kiss motion with his fingers. "I always go back for seconds."

"Try thirds," Charlie said, poking him in the belly. "But he's right. It's super good. I'm feeling the pot roast tonight, though. Honestly, it's a tie."

"Chicken."

"Pot roast."

I held up a hand to cut off their squabbling.

"I'll try a little of both."

They beamed as they shuffled through the line in front of me. Trevor heaped a pile of chicken onto his plate and made a beeline for the potato section, with Charlie fast on his heels. I looked up to see Luke smiling behind the buffet table.

"Hey, Luke. You don't mind me helping with the cats, do you?"

"Of course not! I was hoping you wouldn't cancel. I don't know if we'll see them, but meet me at the side door about half an hour after dinner service. I like to grab all the leftovers I can for them."

"See you then."

I snagged a chicken leg with the tongs before ladling some of the beef onto my plate, organizing them on my plate so they didn't touch. If there was one thing I couldn't stand, it was my food touching. I made my way through the rest of the line and met up with Danny and Charlie at the end.

"Oh, rats. She's at our usual table," Charlie said, tossing her hair to the side. "I can't eat next to Penny. She always makes mean comments."

"We can sit anywhere," Danny said. "Let's go talk to Josh."

Charlie frowned, but followed him over to the table where an older man was sitting. She slapped her tray down and glared at Penny's back. Josh turned and chuckled before glancing up at me.

"You must be the new girl, Eden. I'm Josh. Trevor told me all about you."

"Josh is on the security team," Charlie said, picking up her fork. "He's been here forever."

"I don't know about forever, young lady, but I've been here long enough to know you need to nip this thing you've got with Penny in the butt. No good can come from sniping at one another."

"That's how they get their cardio," Danny said, his mouth full.

Josh rolled his eyes before smiling at me. The lights of the dining room bounced off his bald head.

"Maybe you can talk some sense into them. How are you liking Valewood?"

I paused with my chicken halfway to my mouth and cocked my head to the side.

"I love it here. Everyone is like family. I'm really lucky to be here."

I bit into the leg, surprised at my honesty. There was something about the crew here that made me feel at home. The rosemary in the chicken hit me and I closed my eyes while I chewed. Danny was right. This was amazing.

"Wait till you try the potatoes," Danny said, leaning across the table. "I wouldn't be surprised if I end up as big as Josh here if I keep eating all three meals at the resort."

Josh patted his belly and threw his head back to laugh.

"You can't blame the resort for this. It was hard earned through the years."

The rest of the meal sped by as I listened to their banter. Before I knew it, we were the last people left in the dining hall. I stood up, excited to see the clowder. I planned to call Hannah as soon as I was back in my cabin. Hopefully, I'd have good news for her.

Charlie looked at her watch and let out a yelp.

"Oh geez. I didn't realize it was this late. Wendy's gonna kill me."

I grabbed her tray and put it on top of mine.

"I've got this. Go ahead."

"You're a lifesaver," she said, clapping me on the shoulder before racing across the room. "Talk to you later!"

Danny and Josh were deep in conversation, but they nodded to me as I walked away.

"See you tomorrow," Danny said, before turning his head back to Josh.

"Nice meeting you, Eden. See you around."

I bussed the two trays and looked around the hall. The crew had already cleaned the buffet tables, which meant Luke should be ready. I zipped up my coat and hustled outside, searching for the side door. As I turned the corner, I spotted his thin frame leaning against the building, holding onto an enormous tray.

"Luke, do you need any help?"

He smiled and finished straightening up as I rushed over.

"No, there's not too much in here. Just some leftover meat. Hopefully, they'll like the chicken. The spot where I feed them is over in the trees. Do you have boots on?"

"Yep. Lead the way."

I was finally going to get to meet the cats. The thought made my feet light as we trudged through the snow.

# Chapter Six

Luke was quiet as we walked. I trailed behind him, stepping in the boot prints he left behind to make it easier to get through the snow. I was breathing hard by the time we hit the treeline.

"Cats! Dinner time!"

Luke's shout echoed through the forest and I shivered in place as I looked up at the sky. The moon was almost full and now that my eyes were adjusted, I could see everything clearly in its light. I watched as he put the tray down and started scooping through the snow.

"What are you looking for?" I asked, joining him.

"I don't want them to have to eat off the ground," he said, glancing over his shoulder. "I left a platter last night, but the snow must have blown over it."

I dropped to my knees and helped him scrape away the snow. A loud meow caught my attention, and I turned, surprised to see a brown cat staring at us.

"There you are, girl," Luke said, his voice quiet. "I've got some nice chicken for you. A little beef, too."

She glanced at him before fastening her eyes onto me with a

harsh stare. I gulped, as it felt like she was searching through my soul.

"This is Eden. She's good people," Luke said. "You can trust her."

I looked over at Luke, surprised. He blushed and shrugged his bony shoulders.

"I can tell."

The brown cat moved closed, sniffing intently. I stayed where I was, even though my pants were getting wet in the snow as she inspected me. She blinked slowly and let out another surprising meow.

"What's wrong, girl?" I asked, reaching out to her.

She flattened her ears and backed out of my reach before meowing again. She walked a few steps away towards a bush and turned to me, meowing loudly again.

I exchanged glances with Luke, and he shrugged again.

"I think she wants something, or has something in the bush."

I stood, nearly toppling over in the snow, and walked towards her slowly.

"Is that it?"

She backed out of my reach, but kept staring at the bush. I dropped to my knees again and peered underneath the branches. I could just make out a still, furry form. On no.

"Luke! I think there's a cat in here. I don't know if it's okay."

He made it over to me in a single step and looked at where I was pointing. He let out a low moan.

"Oh no, it's the old gentleman. Oh, buddy."

My fingers went to my mouth as the sides of the cat moved slightly.

"He's alive! Can you grab him?" I asked, tears springing to my eyes.

Luke shifted and glanced at me, his luminous eyes full of pain.

"I can, but I'm super allergic to cats."

"What? You're the one who feeds them?"

"I know. I love them, but I can't touch them. I have terrible asthma and I can't handle their fur."

"I'm sorry, Luke. That's got to be terrible. I'll grab him."

I lay down on my stomach, uncaring that I'd be soaked in a few minutes. Getting this cat out of the bush was far more important. I carefully eased my hands underneath his form and dragged him out. I thought I glimpsed a golden eye as I cradled him to my chest.

"I've got him."

I struggled to my feet and turned around, gasping as I saw what had to be twenty cats grouped around us in a semicircle. The brown cat was at the center, never taking her eyes off of me. A feeling of reverence filled my chest as we made eye contact.

"I'll take care of him. I promise."

I don't know what came over me, but there was no way I was leaving this cat behind. Wild, feral, it didn't matter. He needed help, and I would do whatever it took to keep him safe. The brown cat nodded once.

"Wow. That's kinda baffling," Luke said from his spot a few feet away. "They're completely ignoring all the food."

He was right. The cats were looking at us, ignoring the tray heaped with still warm food. I held the small bundle closer to my chest and looked at Luke.

"I need to get him to my cabin. Is there a vet in town?"

He walked over to the tray and began scooping the food onto the platter.

"There is, but they don't do emergencies. You'll have to wait until morning. Eden, he's the oldest cat in the clowder. You understand that... I hate to say this..."

"No! I don't want to hear that," I said. "I'll keep him warm and take him to the vet at first light."

The tears running down my cheeks felt like fire as the wind picked up. I looked at the cats as they crowded around the platter. I'd expected chaos, but they were so orderly. The smallest cats were eating first, while the bigger ones hung back, watching over them. There was something so touching about it, I almost couldn't tear my eyes away.

The cat in my arms let out a low meow and I snapped back to reality. Right. He needed warmth, and he needed it fast. I started walking back towards the resort, leaving Luke behind. I heard the tray clanging as he jogged to catch up.

"I know you mean well, Eden," he said, his voice choking. "But you have to be prepared. I meant what I said. You're a good person. I can tell. Don't get too attached."

It was far too late for that. Thanks to Hannah's request, I felt attached to the clowder before I'd even met them. Now? I would move heaven and earth to keep them safe.

"I know what you're saying. I have to try."

We were quiet as we hurried through the snow. Luke grabbed my arm as we reached the dining hall.

"Look, I'll grab a few things you might need tonight. He'll need a place to do his business and some food. What cabin are you in?"

"Ten. Thank you, Luke."

"I'll be there in a few minutes."

I walked ahead and made it to my cabin in record time. I flipped on the light and grabbed the remote, cranking the heat. I held the cat close as I walked into the bathroom and grabbed a towel. He'd need a nest of sorts. I had little in my room, and I frowned as I walked back and forth, trying to come up with a solution. A rap on the door startled me.

I was still holding onto the cat as I opened the door and spotted Luke. His arms were full, and he nodded as he bent his head and walked in.

"I grabbed everything I could think of. I found some sand that we use to de-ice the walks and put it in a dish tub. I brought an extra one, too. You could use it as a bed. I don't know if he'll be up for eating, but I brought some bowls you can use for food and water."

Relief spiked through my chest as he put the empty plastic tub down on my desk. It was perfect.

"Thank you, Luke. You've thought of everything! Here's a towel we can put inside of it to soften it for him."

He grinned before taking the towel and using it to line the tub. He stepped back and nodded.

"See if he likes it."

I carefully lowered the cat into the tub and stroked his grizzled head. He opened his eyes briefly, revealing a set of beautiful golden eyes before shutting them tight. Luke cleared his throat and got closer to the door.

"I'm sorry, I really am, but I'd better get out of here. I wish I could do more. Oh! Here's a little food," he said, digging in his pockets. "I can bring more in the morning."

He put the plastic bag full of little bits of meat on the counter and gave me an awkward wave before backing towards the door.

"You're the best, Luke. You can't help your allergies."

"See you in the morning."

He glanced at the tub before walking through the door. I shut it behind him and leaned against it, legs shaking. What on earth was I going to do? Was I even allowed to keep a cat here? What was I going to tell Hannah?

I bit my lip before gathering my courage and walking back to my desk. These worries paled compared to taking care of him.

I dug in my bag and pulled out my favorite scarf. It was fluffy and perfect for keeping him warm.

"Here you go. I wonder if you're Jasper. Hannah mentioned you."

He opened his eyes for a split second, locking into mine and for a second, I swore he answered me with a shaky yes.

I blinked and shook my head. It had been a long day, and it was going to be a long night. I busied myself filling up the small bowls Luke brought. Water went in one, but I paused before filling up the second one with the food from Luke.

I opened the baggie and fished out a small piece of chicken, and walked back over to the tub.

"Jasper? Do you want some meat?"

His eyes remained closed and my shoulders dropped. A cat, especially one this thin, turning down meat? That wasn't a good sign. I dropped it back into the baggie and stored the meat in the fridge. Maybe I could try again later. I washed my hands and dried them before placing the small bowl of water next to the tub. I wasn't sure how he was going to have the strength to reach it, but I wanted him to have access to it, at least.

My next step was calling Hannah. I didn't want to be the one to tell her I'd found Jasper only to follow-up with the fact he was very sick. My stomach lurched as it tied itself into knots. I couldn't put it off. I needed help.

I pulled my cell phone out of my pocket. Hannah would know what to do.

# Chapter Seven

I paced back and forth, playing with the end of my braid, as I waited for Hannah to answer her phone. Hearing her cheerful voice on the other end of the line nearly took me to my knees.

"Hey, Shireen, ope, sorry, Eden. I'm still getting used to using your middle name. Which I love, by the way. How's Valewood?"

I dropped my braid and waved my hand, forgetting for a second she couldn't see me.

"Fine. Well, not really. Hannah, I need help," I said, blurting out the words.

"Okay, Eden. It's okay. Take a deep breath. What's wrong?"

"I went with Luke to feed the cats tonight and we found a cat underneath the bush. I think it might be Jasper."

Her quick intake of breath was followed by a strangled sob.

"Is he?"

"No! No, sorry. He's with me in my cabin. I've got him in a little bed and I've made him warm, but I don't know what to do. There's no emergency vet near here and my car is in the shop."

"Oh! Thank goodness he's alive! I can't believe he let you bring him inside."

I looked over at Jasper's slumbering form and shook my head.

"He had little choice. What should I do?"

"One second. I'm going to get Anastasia and patch her in. Hang on, Razzy. Yes, it's about Jasper."

The rest of what she was saying to her cat was cut off as she put me on hold. I started pacing again, thoughts racing ahead of me. Hannah talked to Razzy like she could understand what was going on. I thought back to the semi-circle the clowder made, and my feet came to a stop. Was it possible they really could understand what was going on?

Had I completely misjudged how intelligent cats were? From where I was standing, it was clear I was severely lacking in feline knowledge.

"Okay, Eden? Are you here?"

Hearing Hannah's voice yanked me back to reality, and I nodded.

"I'm here."

"Hello, dear," Anastasia's warm voice came through the line.

Instant calm flowed over me and I blinked in shock.

"I'm so glad I called you, Hannah. Hi Anastasia. I'm so sorry to bother you this late at night."

"Nonsense. This is important. Are you standing next to Jasper?"

I moved closer to my desk and peeked inside the bed I'd made for the older cat. He hadn't moved, but his sides were still going up and down.

"I am now. What should I do? I don't have any veterinarian skills."

"You won't need them, dear. Just an open mind and an open heart. You have the necklace I gave you, right?"

For a second, I couldn't compute what she was asking. What on earth did the necklace have to do with anything?

"Yes."

I patted my chest where it hung, forgotten since the day I'd put it on.

"I want you to put your hand on Jasper and close your eyes, okay?"

I followed Anastasia's command and closed my eyes. I wasn't

sure about this, but right now, it was my only option. It wouldn't hurt, right? Was she going to use the necklace to forge some sort of connection? I felt so disoriented I could be in a different galaxy than they were.

"Okay, I'm doing that."

The line went quiet and for a horrible second, I thought the call dropped. A warmth started in my chest, centered on the stone hanging there from its cord. My eyes flew open as the feeling traveled down my arm, into my hand. Jasper's thin side stilled for a split second before inflating with a deep breath. Yep, it appeared I was right about the whole necklace connection thing. How strange was this?

"There," Anastasia said, her voice flowing like honey through the line. "I would still take him to the vet in the morning, but he will be okay tonight."

I slowly stroked Jasper's side. His whiskers curled up in what looked like a smile. What had just happened? My brain immediately wanted to discount what I was seeing, but I couldn't. I didn't know what had happened. I didn't care. All that mattered was Jasper looked better.

"Eden? Are you there?"

"I'm here. Sorry, I just..."

"I understand," Hannah said. "Just believe. It makes it easier."

"If you need anything else, dear, please call me. Any time, it doesn't matter," Anastasia said, her voice filled with exhaustion. "Callie, be patient. One second, my love. I need to go now. Goodbye, Hannah. We'll talk soon."

There was a click, and I heard a third voice on the line. It was small, but definitely feminine.

"Is he going to be okay, mama?"

"Yes, Razzy. Anastasia said he would be."

I dropped my phone and backed away like it had bitten me. Roaring filled my ears as I sank down to the floor on my knees. I pressed my head into the floor and tried to take a deep breath, but it got stuck in my chest. Was I dreaming?

"Eden?"

I could hear Hannah's voice faintly, and I came back to my senses. I picked my phone up with two fingers and held it back to my ear.

"I'm here. Uh…"

"Get some rest. Trust me, it's the best thing you can do. I'll be here if you need anything. And Eden?"

"Yes?"

"You're not going around the bend. You're going to have some questions. When you're ready, I'll try to answer them. If I can't, Anastasia will help. It's going to be okay. Please give Jasper a kiss for me."

"And me," the small voice piped up again.

I heard a deeper voice in the background, but it didn't sound like Ben. My mind whirled as I tried to form words.

"Thanks, Hannah."

I ended the call and slid it away from me. The roaring in my ears was gone, but my brain felt stretched somehow. Hannah was right. I needed sleep. Here I was, imagining I could hear cats, and that Hannah was talking to them. Answering them, even.

A laugh burst out of my chest, startling me. I clapped my hand over my mouth and shakily got to my feet, eyeing my phone like it was a snake. Was I losing my mind? I picked up the phone and put it on the charger, and walked into the bathroom. I stared at my reflection in the mirror. My face was pale, but I didn't look any different. No devil horns had sprouted out of my head. I snorted and leaned forward to wash my face, using cold water to make sure I was awake. Ouch. Yep, I was.

I dried my face off and folded the towel carefully, avoiding my own eyes in the mirror. A thought popped into my head and I dragged the necklace out of my shirt. Once Anastasia had given it to me, I'd worn it, but practically forgot it existed. The stone looked the same and felt the same. Why had it gotten warm? Could Anastasia use it to spy on me? No, that sounded downright paranoid. She wasn't that type of person. Right? I tucked it back into my shirt and groaned, making a face at myself in the mirror.

I walked back to the kitchenette and opened the fridge before realizing it only held the food I was saving for the cat and half a sandwich. I closed it with a huff and walked over to the desk to peek at Jasper. He was in the same position, but he looked happier somehow. I stroked his brindle fur and cleared my throat.

"You're going to be okay, Jasper. I'll take care of you. I promise."

I paused, half expecting him to wake and speak, but he slept soundly, sides rising and falling predictably. I shook my head and walked towards the bed. Maybe I'd imagined the whole thing, and I was just overreacting. I flipped on the television before grabbing for my pajamas. It was earlier than my normal bedtime, but the only thing I wanted to do was crawl beneath the covers and forget what had just happened. I quickly undressed and dove under the blankets.

The drone of the television did little to distract my spinning mind, and I caught myself chewing on the end of my braid, something I hadn't done since I was a child. I ripped it out of my mouth.

"Geez, get a hold of yourself."

I flipped the end of my braid over my shoulder, safely out of reach, and spread my hands on the covers, looking at my fingers. The scar on my left ring finger I'd gotten when I was five and determined to help my mother in the kitchen. The thumbnail on the right hand that never wanted to grow properly. I was myself, but why did I feel so different?

I groaned and flipped off the television. Maybe reading would help. I got out of bed and walked over to the wardrobe. I'd brought a single well-worn paperback that I'd read countless times, but it felt like coming home as my hands closed around it.

"Do you like books, Jasper?" I asked as I crawled back into bed. "I can read it out loud for you."

I snorted as I realized how silly I must sound. But maybe reading aloud would help corral my thoughts. I settled back onto the pillows and opened the book.

"I found this book at a garage sale when I was twelve, Jasper. It was only five cents. My mother didn't approve of fiction, but I bought it when she was busy talking to someone else. I hid it in my room, under my bed, and I'd read it at night with a flashlight. Heck, I could probably read it from memory. I've read it so many times. It's a great story, all about a woman who solves mysteries in her little hometown of St. Mary Mead. I think you'll get a kick out of her."

A smile came over my face as I settled into the familiar story. By the time I made it to the end of the first chapter, my eyes were heavy. I clicked off the lights and turned onto my side.

"Good night, Jasper. I hope you feel better and sleep well."

My eyes closed and as I slipped under, I thought I heard a soft voice, wishing me the same, but I was probably dreaming.

# Chapter Eight

The room was pitch black when I woke, gasping for breath. I'd spent the entire night dreaming of being just out of reach of something I was chasing. I never knew what it was, just that it was vital I catch it.

"Oh, good. You're awake. Would you mind telling me how I got here?"

I stilled as I heard a soft male voice inside my room. Memories of the past night came flooding back as I blinked furiously. Okay, maybe I was still asleep. Yeah, this had to be one of those dreams within a dream thing. Right?

"Hello?" I asked, my voice rising to a squeak at the very end.

"Are your ears working? I asked how I got here."

The soft voice had a cranky edge to it now, reminding me of a grumpy old man. My lips quirked as I rolled out of bed and put my feet on the cold floor. Hmmm. That was strange. Usually in dreams, I never felt cold.

I padded over to my desk, flipped on the light, and peered inside the plastic tub, where a very belligerent looking cat lay curled up in my scarf.

"Hello. I'm Eden. Are you Jasper?"

The cat sighed, never breaking eye contact with me.

"I finally run into another person who can talk to cats and she keeps saying hello. Just my luck."

"Wow, this is one wild dream," I said, reaching a hand out to him. "Do you mind if I pet you?"

The golden eyes glaring at me narrowed into slits.

"If you must. I would still like an answer to my question."

I gently rubbed under his chin, and a rusty sounding purr came from deep within his chest. His golden eyes looked startled, and he stopped purring.

"I'm sorry. I found you last night when I went with Luke to bring food to the clowder. You were underneath a bush. A brown cat led me to you and I brought you home with me. When I wake up, I'm going to take you to the veterinarian to make sure you're okay."

He coughed out another rusty purr, and I was pretty sure he was smirking at me.

"Doll, you're already awake. I'm going to have a word with Fig. I can't believe she sold me out like that. And I ain't going to the vet. No, thank you. I'm fine."

He struggled to his feet, but his legs shook and he immediately crumpled back into the towel at the bottom of the tub. I reached for his side, stroking his fur gently as he breathed fast.

"How strange. You're calling the brown cat by the same name Hannah does. Please, don't get up again. I'm really worried about you. Anastasia said you'd be fine through the night, so hopefully when I'm done with this dream, you'll be okay and I'll get you into town. I don't know how I'm going to do that, not yet anyway. My car broke down. Maybe I can borrow someone's car."

"Anastasia? I know that name. Again, girly, you're not dreaming. And I'm not going to the vet."

We glared at each other until a knock at my door startled me. I shook my finger at Jasper.

"Yes. You are. One second."

I opened the door and shivered as cold air tackled me. My thin sleep tee felt like it was made of tissue paper.

"Is he okay? I'm sorry to bug you so early, but we start breakfast prep before dawn. I saw your light on," Luke said, his breath visible in the frosty morning air.

I blinked at him for a second as everything came crashing in on me at once. I really wasn't dreaming. I grabbed the side of the door and held on for dear life. I needed to keep it together.

"He's alive. I've got to borrow someone's car to take him into town. I forgot mine's still in the shop. I never heard yesterday about what's wrong with it."

Luke dug into his pockets and grinned.

"You can take mine. It's the old Civic parked in the employee lot. It's not the nicest, but it's full of gas."

I wrapped my hands around the keys, the cold metal biting into my skin.

"Thank you, Luke. You're the best! I wonder what time the clinic opens?"

He glanced at his watch.

"They'll be open in thirty minutes. I've taken my mom's cat in and dropped her off before work. Do you know how to get to the clinic?"

I waved a hand, desperate the shut the door so I could have my mental breakdown in peace.

"I'll find it. I've kept you long enough. As soon as I get back, I'll let you know how he is."

"See you, Eden!"

He turned and jogged through the snow, his lanky form awkward as he plowed through a drift. I shut the door firmly and put my forehead against it before taking a deep breath.

Point one, I was not dreaming. Point two, I had just had a conversation with a cat. Point three, apparently Hannah and Anastasia could also talk to cats. Had I fallen into some strange witchcraftian plot?

I clapped a hand over my mouth in horror as I heard my mother's voice in my head say the last part. Hannah and Anastasia were the nicest people I'd ever met, and they certainly weren't witches. No, this was something else.

I heard a plaintive meow from my desk and shook my head. I would have to reschedule my breakdown. Right now, I had a sick cat who needed my help. I shoved myself away from the door and walked back to Jasper, putting the keys down next to him.

"You let in all the cold air," he said, fidgeting to get comfortable. "It's rare that I get to enjoy my creature comforts. I can't get too soft. I suppose I'll be back out in it soon enough."

"Not if I have any say in the matter, Mr. Jasper. I need to get dressed and we're going to the vet. No arguments."

I spun on my heel and marched over to my closet, pulled out my warmest hoodie and jeans, and put them on the bed. I popped into the bathroom to brush my teeth and made a face as I realized how messy my hair was. I'd left it in a braid, as I always did, but it was frizzing around my head in a cloud, half of it hanging down while the other half rioted. Wonderful. The dark circles under my eyes confirmed my restless night.

I spit out my toothpaste and started undoing my braid, fingers getting caught in my tangles. I didn't have time for this. I finished undoing the braid and left it loose. I'd redo it later.

It tickled my arms as I hurried back into the main room and pulled my hoodie over my sleep tee. I searched through my closet until I found a beanie and clapped it over my hair, hoping it would at least help contain the wildness. In five minutes, I was dressed and trying to figure out how to transport Jasper to Luke's car.

"I suppose I can wrap your tub in my coat. That would block the chill until I can get you into the car," I said, snapping my fingers.

"What now? I said we're not going to the vet. I will not be poked and prodded!"

"Yeah, yeah. You're going."

His whiskers quirked to the side as he titled his head.

"Huh. I had you pegged as a pushover. Looks like someone's a little feistier than I thought."

"And don't you forget it. Okay, I'm going to wrap you up. I'll keep you as warm as I can, okay? I'll try not to jostle you."

I carefully laid my coat over the tub, blocking my view of Jasper, grabbed Luke's keys and walked to the door, snagging my bag on the way.

The snow crunched under my feet as I made my way to the employee lot. There were only a few cars there, and luckily, Luke's was the only Civic. I opened the door and eased the tub into the passenger seat.

"I'm going to leave the coat over you until I get the heat on. Have you ever been in a car?"

The muffled yowl from under my coat could have several meanings. I yanked the door shut and put the keys in.

"Heat... heat... where's the heat? There you are," I said, twisting the knob to full blast. "Oh, thank goodness this is an automatic. I didn't even ask. Alright, Mr. Jasper. We're on our way."

I was on the highway before I realized I'd forgotten my phone and didn't know where the clinic was. Well, Valewood was small. Maybe I'd luck out and find some signs. The chill in the car eased and while I waited at the stop sign, I slid my coat back a little. Jasper's grizzled head popped out and if his eyes were any sign, if he'd been stronger, he might have scratched me.

"Don't be angry, Jasper. I have to make sure you're okay."

The slitted golden eyes never left my face until I pulled my eyes away and focused on the road. The sign said Valewood, two miles and I breathed a sigh of relief.

"I'm fine. Really. We can turn around. The clowder's probably worried sick about me. I need to make sure the patrols are going out like they should. It's hard work keeping everyone fed, especially with all the snow this year. The wild game is scarce. If it wasn't for Luke..."

He trailed off and hung his head. My heart twinged painfully in my chest. I couldn't imagine how difficult their lives were. If I had any say in the matter, the entire clowder would live in my cabin, warm as little snug bugs, and well fed.

"They'll be okay. Let's see what the vet says. With any luck, you're fit as a fiddle. Have you been to a vet before?"

I glanced over just in time to see a look of longing pass over Jasper's face.

"Once. A long time ago. There was a girl," he said, looking at me. "She was a lot like you. Had the same gift. She took me in and had me checked out. I had some sort of operation. She said I'd been neutered."

He paused, shuddering, and quirked his whiskers before speaking again.

"Never wanted kits anyway, so I guess it's fine. I never thought I'd been in the position of going back to a vet, though."

"You said gift. What do you mean?"

"Do you think everyone can talk to cats? I've walked this earth for many years and I've only found three. Well, four if you count the woo-woo redhead. There must be something in the water around here."

I snorted as I realized he was likely talking about Anastasia.

"You think I'm gifted?"

"I think you're something," he said, curling into a ball. "Wake me when you're ready to have me act like a pincushion."

I pulled into Valewood and began searching the store fronts, looking for a sign for the vet's clinic. I turned off the main road and headed down a side street, spotting a gas station. They'd be able to help. I pulled in and left the engine running.

"I'll be right back."

Jasper was silent, and I frowned as I shut the door. Our talk must have worn him out. I needed to hurry. I ducked inside and smiled at the woman at the register. Her round face lit with a smile as she spotted me.

"Can I help you, honey?"

"Hi. Could you tell me where the vet clinic is?"

"Sure thing. That street you came in on? Take that down another two blocks and turn left. It will be the gray building on the left. Can't miss it."

"Thanks!"

I waved and darted back out, hopping into the car.

"We're not far, Jasper. Hang in there."

I followed the directions and sure enough, there was no missing the sign for the Valewood vet clinic. I pulled the coat back over the tub and headed inside, gripping it to my chest. A chime sounded as I walked in and I spotted a young girl behind the desk. Her strawberry blond hair shone under the bright lights.

"Can I help you?"

"Hi. I don't have an appointment, but I found a cat last night, and he's in rough shape. Can you help?"

"Of course. We can squeeze him in right now, before the morning rush. I'll have you fill out the paperwork while I find the doctor."

She grabbed a clipboard and shoved a few sheets of paper into it before motioning me to follow her. She pointed into a small room and held out the clipboard.

"It should only be a few minutes."

I gave her a grateful smile and put Jasper's tub down on the metal table in the center of the room, peeking under the coat.

"Jasper, we're here. Be good. Please."

He raised himself up and looked around the room, his thin shoulders quaking.

"I don't like the smell here. I don't like it all."

I wanted nothing more than to pick him up and cradle him to my chest, but I couldn't risk hurting him. I settled for stroking his head for a minute until he calmed down.

"You'll be okay. I won't let them hurt you."

His golden eyes fixed on mine and something unspoken passed between us. My heart felt warm, and I struggled to keep my eyes from tearing up. He nodded once and put his head back down. I paced before remembering I needed to fill out the forms.

I jotted down my name and his, but that's about all I knew. I wasn't sure how old he was, and other than his description of visiting a vet once, I didn't know his history. I put the clipboard down on the table and drummed my fingers on the metal.

The door burst open and a tall woman entered, her brows crinkled.

"I didn't get your name, sorry. I'm Dr. Ruth. What do we have here?"

"I'm Eden Brooks. I've got Jasper. He's an older cat who lives out by the Valewood resort in the feral colony. I found him last night. I'm not sure what's wrong with him."

Her light green eyes were serious as she gently reached into the tub. Jasper's eyes blazed, but I shook my head and he went limp, accepting her touch. Her voice crooned as she carefully put him on the table.

"My, my, you are an older gentleman, aren't you? Okay, I'm going to need to do a few things. He seems to like you, so if you can hold him, that will make it easier."

I nodded and put my hand on Jasper's head as she grabbed a thermometer. I winced as she set to work, all business. She pulled a syringe out of her coat pocket and focused on his leg. I turned away as she drew blood. Jasper was silent, but tense. I knew this wasn't easy for him.

"Okay, sit tight. I'm going to have the lab look at this. From what I can tell, he's dehydrated, and he's missed way too many meals. He needs an IV. I'll get that all set up while we run the tests. Please, have a seat."

I stroked his side as she left the room. His words about feeding the clowder came back to me.

"You've been giving up your food for the other cats, haven't you?"

His eye cracked open slightly before closing again.

"They're young. I'm not. It's only right."

I bit my lip to keep from crying as I kept stroking him. No matter what the vet came back with, there was no way this cat was ever going to go hungry again. Not if I could help it.

# Chapter Nine

Jasper's baleful stare never left my face on the entire drive back to the resort. I knew this because I kept sneaking glances over at him. Even if I hadn't, it's entirely possible I would've felt him boring a hole through me.

"Why, in this modern era, do they insist on taking a cat's temperature that way?"

"I don't know. I'm sorry. But it had to be done. Are you feeling any better?"

A sniff was the only answer I'd gotten. The vet assured me that although Jasper was getting up there, overall, he was healthy, given his condition. I'd been given special food that would help him put weight back on, and strict instructions on how to make sure he was getting enough food and water. I intended to follow them to the letter, no matter how much fuss Jasper put up.

I slowed as I turned into the resort and came to a stop in the middle of the road. Flashing lights were everywhere, and my heart skipped a beat before racing. What on earth happened while I was gone?

Jasper's eyes softened as he struggled to stand.

"Are you okay? What's wrong?"

I snapped out of my panic and reached a hand to stroke his fur.

"I don't know. There's an ambulance and several police cars. Oh, I hope no one was hurt."

I crept forward and parked in the employee lot before turning to Jasper.

"I'm going to leave the car on so you can get some heat. Let me check this out before I take you back to the cabin."

"I'm feeling much better. I need to get back to the clowder."

I shut the car door and turned to face him.

"No. You're still not out of the woods," I said, holding up a hand to block his protest. "I know you want to get back to your people, but you need to recover. You're stuck with me, mister."

A creaky purr started deep in his chest and for a second, I could swear he was laughing. Could a cat laugh?

"I'm definitely not in the woods, because that's where I want to be. I know what you mean," he said, stretching as his back legs shook. "Maybe you're right. But only for another day. I need to get back."

I stroked his head and shook my head.

"We'll see about that. I'll be right back."

I got out of the car and shut the door carefully behind me, even though I knew Jasper wasn't in any shape to go bounding past. I trusted him, but I knew how much he wanted to go home. I wiped my sweaty palms on my jeans and eyed the police cars. A commotion by the front doors of the resort drew my attention, and I watched as paramedics guided a cart through them.

My feet moved with no input from my brain and I jumped as a familiar voice rang out.

"Eden? Oh my gosh, there you are! Where were you?"

Charlie's familiar face bounced into view, but my attention drifted to a tall man leaning against a sedan. His eyes narrowed as he watched us. I didn't recognize him.

"Charlie, hush. Who is that?"

She started looking around wildly, her multi-colored ponytail swinging.

"Who? Where?"

She didn't lower her voice any, and I winced as the man levered himself off his car and started in our direction.

"Never mind. I guess I'll find out in a few seconds, anyway. What happened?"

She grabbed my arm and leaned close, finally whispering.

"A guest died. At first, we weren't sure what was going on. I knocked on your cabin door, but you weren't anywhere to be found. Where were you, Eden?"

"Yes, that's a question I'd like the answer to as well," the man said, placing his hands on his narrow hips, his fingers knocking into the badge secured there.

Now that he was closer, I could make out the details on his face. In any other situation, he'd be what I considered attractive. His light brown hair fell softly onto his forehead, and the sides grazed his ears. He needed a haircut. My eyes went to his, noticing that minus the look of suspicion aimed at me, they were a beautiful blue, the color of a glacial lake. A smattering of freckles brushed across both cheeks, joining across his nose. What was I doing?

"Eden? Are you okay?"

I blinked and tried to smile, but it came out shaky.

"I'm fine. Sorry. I was at the veterinary clinic in town. I have a receipt, if you don't believe me," I said, half turning to the car.

"The vet? I didn't think you had a... Oh, wait, that pet?" Charlie asked, glancing at me with another question in her eyes, this one silent.

She had my back, and was prepared to lie for me if I needed her to. I smiled at her, appreciating her loyalty.

"I don't. Well, I guess I do now. Kinda. It's hard to explain."

"I'm all ears, Miss... I didn't catch your last name," the man said.

"Sorry. Eden Brooks. Well, my actual name is Shireen Brooks, but I don't like my first name, so I changed it to my middle name. I didn't do any paperwork, though. Will that get me in trouble? Should I need legally change it? Am I breaking the law?"

Great. Now I was babbling. His blue eyes thawed, and one side of his lips quirked up. It wasn't a smile, but he no longer looked like he was considering slapping handcuffs on me. At least I didn't think he was considering it.

"I think we can let that slide. I'm Detective Ethan Rhodes. Relax, I don't think you hurt anyone. I was more interested in asking if you saw anything. What time did you go to the vet?"

"Ethan Rhodes?" I asked, voice jumping so high I had to clear my throat. "Hannah Murphy mentioned you when she helped me get this job. She said you were nice."

"You know Hannah and Ben?" he asked, tilting his head to the side.

"Yes," I asked, shoulders slumping as I watched the residual wariness flee his eyes. "Ben and Hannah saved my life."

I winced before I glanced at Charlie, uncertain if this was the right moment to lay my heavy past on her. I really didn't want to tell Ethan the details, either, truth be told. I wanted my past to stay firmly buried. Where it belonged.

Ethan's eyes softened a little more. Charlie's lips moved to the side, and I knew she had questions. I just didn't want to answer them. Not right now. I needed to change the subject.

"You said a guest was hurt?" I asked, turning towards Charlie. "Who was it?"

"I don't know," Charlie said, running her hands through her hair. "One of Penny's girls radioed the front desk in a panic and I called 9-1-1. From the look of that gurney, though, I'd say whoever it was is more than hurt."

I glanced over her shoulder and my eyes goggled as I realized the person on top of the stretcher was encased in a dark plastic shield. Oh no. I put my hand over my heart and looked at Ethan. His lips flattened as he nodded his head.

"Yes. They are deceased."

My brain whirred as I put all the pieces together. If reading murder mysteries had taught me anything, it was that detectives didn't get sent out to an accident unless there was a suspicion of foul play. Ethan was a detective. Did we have a murderer at this resort?

My hands shook, and I gripped my fingers together, hoping it would pass.

"What time did it happen?"

"That's what I'm trying to figure out. From the amount of blood in the room, it's clear this wasn't a simple injury."

Charlie's pale skin went a shade lighter, and I closed my eyes as the concrete under my feet heaved up. Well, maybe it wasn't the concrete. I felt a firm hand encircle my arm, tangling in my hair.

"I'm sorry. I shouldn't have said that. Are you okay, Miss Brooks?"

I nodded, unable to speak, and looked into Ethan's eyes, searching for something. I wasn't sure what I was looking for.

"I'm fine, too," Charlie said, her eyes bouncing between us like she was at a tennis match. "In case anyone was wondering."

Ethan cleared his throat and gently untangled his fingers from my hair as he released my arm.

"What time did you leave the resort?"

I gathered my hair and attempted to tame it while the wind whipped through the parking lot. My waist long strands were going to be helplessly snarled. I twisted it around into a bun before remembering I was wearing a stocking hat. Geez, I was really slipping. I let it fall as I answered.

"Right before seven. The vet's office opened then. Luke dropped by my cabin. He can vouch for me."

"Why did you need to go to the vet?" Ethan asked, glancing over his shoulder as the paramedics moved the body into the ambulance.

"I was helping Luke feed the cats," I said, pointing towards the woods. "There's a group of feral cats that live there. Anyway, we found an older cat underneath a bush and I brought him back to my cabin. I wasn't sure he'd make it through the night. I hope Mr. Marsburg won't be angry that I had a cat inside. I didn't know what else to do."

"He won't mind," Charlie said, shoving her hands in her pockets. "He's cool like that."

Ethan smiled and his freckled nose crinkled in the cutest gesture I'd seen in a long time.

"That's very sweet of you. Is the cat going to be okay?"

"I hope so. He's very thin and dehydrated. I need to get him inside. I left Luke's car running, so he'd have heat while he waited. I hope I'm not burning up all of Luke's gas."

I glanced over my shoulder at the car.

"Just one more question," Ethan said. "Did you see anything when you left? You didn't go into the main part of the resort?"

"That's two questions," Charlie said, cracking her gum.

Ethan ignored her, his eyes never leaving mine.

"No. I saw nothing. I went from my cabin to the parking lot and then to the vet and straight back. I'm sorry."

He gave me a half smile and fished into his pocket, pulling out a card.

"Here's my number. If you think of anything, or if you hear anything, please call."

I pocketed the card and nodded.

"I will."

He nodded and turned to leave.

"I will too," Charlie said, leaning forward as Ethan walked away.

He waved but didn't turn back to us. She rounded on me and grabbed both my arms.

"Holy smokes, I could literally see the chemistry between the two of you. And look at all this hair," she said, grabbing a hank from behind my shoulder. "I knew it was long, but oh my gosh, it's amazing."

I patted my hair, grimacing as my fingers caught in it.

"I don't know about that. Right now, I'd love to chop it all off. I may have to if I don't get it untangled. I need to get Jasper back to the cabin."

"I'll help," Charlie said, looping her arm through mine. "And while we walk, we can talk about Detective McHotterson over there and how much he's into you."

My cheeks heated painfully as I stopped by Luke's car and opened the door.

"Sorry, Jasper. I didn't think it was going to take that long. Are you okay?"

"I'm fine. What's going on? I smell death."

I swallowed hard and glanced at Charlie as she leaned into the small space next to me.

"Is that him? Oh, he looks so sweet. And the way he meowed when you asked him a question. It's like he was talking."

Reality hit me like a ton of bricks. I was talking to a cat in front of my new friend. He was answering me, but she only heard meows. Holy moly, was I losing my mind? I shook off my panic and realized I was letting all the cold air into the vehicle. Catching a chill was the last thing Jasper needed. I shrugged off my coat and draped it over him, scooping up the tub.

"Could you turn off the engine for me?" I asked Charlie, unwilling to make eye contact with her.

"Sure. Anything else you need me to grab?"

"Oh. Um. That food. That would be great. He's on a special diet until he recovers."

"Geez, I bet that wasn't cheap," Charlie said, pocketing the keys and grabbing the food before slamming the car door shut.

It wasn't, but I wouldn't complain. Whatever it took to get Jasper back to health, I would pay it. I shut out my fears as I walked back to my cabin, half-listening to Charlie rattle on about Detective Ethan Rhodes. A brief spark burned in my chest, but I shook my head. Now was not the time to think about romance.

# Chapter Ten

Once we were safely in my room, I turned to Charlie, focusing on her while I put Jasper's tub down on the counter. She put a tentative finger towards his muzzle, but pulled it back when he gave her the stink eye.

"Sorry. I wasn't trying to be rude. Are you sure you're okay?" Charlie asked, narrowing her eyes at me. "You seem really jumpy."

"Well, it looks like someone was just killed, so yeah, I guess I'm a little jumpy."

I pulled the sleeves of my hoodie over my fingers and busied myself, checking Jasper's water, hanging my coat, puttering around the kitchenette. Pretty much anything I could think of to keep from meeting her eyes. I didn't trust myself not to break down. Everything was reminding me of him. I'd sworn I would not waste another second or another tear on Adam Caldwell. Right as I thought about his name, the tears started. I flung off my beanie, aiming for the bed, missing, and started attacking the tangles in my hair.

"Whoa, whoa. It's okay. I'm sorry. I was prying, and I shouldn't have been. You'll tell me when you're ready. Stop. Your hair is way too pretty to treat it like that. Here, sit on the bed, and I'll brush it out for you. I always wished for a sister so I could do things like this, but all I got was a lousy brother who liked to keep his hair so short you could see his scalp."

I laughed as Charlie dashed to the bathroom, rooting around for something. She appeared, holding a comb up to the sky.

"Got it. Now, sit and talk to me. Or don't. Whichever, it's up to you."

She thumped on the bed and I dragged my feet over to it, sitting on the edge gingerly while she flung herself into the middle.

"Ooo, you've got one of the soft mattresses, too. I swear some of these beds must have come from an institution. They're so hard, if you tried to bounce a quarter off it, it would likely end up on the moon. For reals."

I listened to Charlie's harmless rambling while she gently combed through my hair. My eyes shut, remembering how my mother used to detangle my hair when I was young. I'd done the same thing for my sisters. A few more tears leaked out, and I back-handed them away, hoping Charlie wouldn't notice.

She might not have, but Jasper did. I spotted his little head peeking out of his dish tub. I gave him a watery smile and a thumbs up. What must he think of me?

"How long have you been growing your hair? It's honestly incredible. I don't see any split ends either. It must take you ages to take care of it."

Now there was a safe topic. I cleared my throat.

"Honestly? I just use shampoo and a little conditioner. I only need to wash it once a week. I keep it in a braid or up in a bun most of the time. I've been meaning to get it cut, but every time I go to make an appointment, I lose my courage."

Charlie leaned closer, resting her chin on my shoulder.

"You would dare cut this beautiful mane? Or, I guess, if you do, you could donate it. They could make wigs for five people from this lot."

She settled back and kept working on my tangles. I zoned out for a few minutes, soothed by the gentle repetitive motion of the comb working its way through my hair. My mouth opened, and the truth came spilling out.

"I dated a murderer."

The comb stopped, and I clapped my hand to my mouth, shocked. I turned to face Charlie, who sat there, holding the comb up, a blank look on her face. I held up a hand.

"Well, I guess we weren't dating anymore when he killed someone. But he took me hostage and tried to kill me. I'm sorry I broke down earlier. I'm working on it. Seeing the cop cars brought everything back."

"And this Hannah girl, and what's his name saved you?"

"Ben. Ben Walsh. Yes, they did," I said, hugging my knees to my chest and resting my forehead on them.

"Well, the next time I see them, remind me to buy them a drink. I assume this murderer is locked up somewhere?"

I nodded, feeling lighter.

"He is. His trial is coming up, though. It happened a few months ago. I'll need to testify soon."

"Don't worry," Charlie said, patting my back. "I'll go with you. You don't have to do it alone."

I spun, surprised.

"Really? You barely know me."

"Meh. I could tell when you walked into the resort we were gonna be besties. I've got a sense like that. Enough of focusing on the past. You can tell me the gory details another time. What about this cute detective? Did you see his eyes?"

I waved my hand and turned around, hoping she didn't catch the color flooding into my cheeks.

"Let's not. What happened this morning?"

"Oh. Are you sure you're okay with talking about it?"

"I'm fine. What happened?"

"Do you want me to braid your hair now? I think I've got all the tangles out."

"Sure. You said something about one of Penny's girls found something in a room?"

"Yay, I love braiding. Okay, so here's what happened," she said, gathering all my hair into her fist. "Jemma, she's in housekeeping, radioed me, screaming her head off. At first, I thought there was something wrong with the radio and it was malfunctioning. Anyway, once I got her to stop screaming, she said she walked into Room 413 and saw blood. Everywhere. She slammed the door and called for help. I called the cops and got everyone rounded up and outside. It was probably another half hour until you showed up. I knocked on your door, but you didn't answer. I was worried sick."

"Who's staying in Room 413?"

Charlie's hands stilled and she let out a gasp.

"Oh my gosh. I didn't even think to look. I just went into autopilot."

I swiveled my head, only to get a gentle smack on my back.

"Don't move. I've almost got this done. Here, you can take my phone. I've got the portal for the resort on there. My access code is 1111."

I snorted as I typed in her code.

"No hacker's gonna stop you, huh?"

"Hey, I've got enough passwords to remember. Besides, who would want to steal my phone? There, it's the app with the big V."

I tapped on the icon and waited while it loaded. A login screen appeared.

"What's your login?"

"My last name, Granger, and 1111."

Her voice trailed off into a giggle as I rolled my eyes, typing in the password.

"Okay. I'm in. What now?"

"Go to bookings, then manage. You'll see a pull-down menu. Scroll down until you get to 413."

I followed her instructions and waited for the room information to load.

"It says it's for three nights, and for a couple by the name of Brad and Sherry Youngstown."

"Keep scrolling. Do you have a hair tie? I'm done."

I held up my left wrist, and she worked the hair tie off while I scrolled down.

"Oh, wow! You can see the driver's license from the person who booked the room. That's cool. Wait..."

I peered closer at the phone and my stomach dropped. I knew that face. I'd just seen it the day before.

"There! I'm done. Eden? You've gone white. What is it?"

"This is the couple that got into a fight with Penny when they checked in," I said, holding the phone up to her face. "I know that's him. Oh gosh, I wonder which one of them it was on the stretcher. I think they were celebrating their anniversary. I wonder what happened? They seemed so nice, minus the fact they were really mad they didn't get a suite. He threatened Penny. It was intense."

Charlie's eyes got big as she pulled the phone away from her face so she could see it.

"Really?"

"Yeah. I think it shook Wendy up. I'm surprised she said nothing."

Charlie waved her hand and shrugged.

"She was more than ready to go home last night. I barely got a goodbye out of her," Charlie said, stifling a yawn.

I looked at the time on her phone and patted her arm.

"Charlie, you'd better go get some sleep. You've been up all night, and it's already almost nine. Shoot! I need to get to work."

I jumped up and swung the braid over my shoulder. Charlie had done a great job. I hadn't expected it to be in a fishtail.

"Fine, but you have to tell me what you find out. I don't think Mr. Marsburg will be upset if you call off today. The resort is going to be chaos," Charlie said, stifling another yawn as she crawled out of my bed. "Stuff like this never happens here. I bet we'll all get the day off. Well, minus housekeeping."

"I'll meet you before dinner. Thank you for the braid. It looks incredible. I might have you help me more often."

She grinned brightly, flicking her multi-colored hair over her shoulder.

"Any time. That was fun. See you later. Oh, Eden? Be safe. It might just be a domestic fight that turned ugly, or we might have a murderer on the loose."

I stilled as she waved and closed the door, leaving me alone with Jasper. I turned to the cat and tilted my head.

"You really can talk, right? I'm not just imagining things?"

"I can talk. And so can that girl. My ears hurt."

"Hey, she's nice. And yes, she's a chatterbox, but she's the closest thing to a friend I have. That's weird. She just heard meows while I can understand you. Are you feeling better?"

Jasper's golden eyes shone at me as I tucked him in.

"I'm fine. I want to check on the clowder, though. Can you take me there this afternoon?"

I paused and considered it. I could take my lunch break and head into the woods. The wind blew outside, rattling the window. I shook my head.

"I'll go, but you're staying right here. I'll check on them and report back. Deal?"

He grumbled under his breath, moving the towel I'd just put around him.

"Fine. Quit fussing."

I stroked his head and smiled as his whiskers turned up. He might play at being a grump, but I knew there was a soft heart buried under that tabby fur.

"I'll fuss if I want to. Now, I've got to report for duty and see what I can find out. I never expected this on my second day at work."

"She was right about one thing," Jasper said, settling himself into a comfortable spot. "Be careful."

I nodded and grabbed my beanie off the floor, pulling it over my ears.

"See you later."

I closed the door and walked through the snow towards the resort. The flashing lights were gone, but it didn't feel peaceful. I shuddered as the wind blew right through my coat. Something still felt off.

## Chapter Eleven

Wendy's panicky eyes met mine as I walked in the front door, stomping a bit to get the snow off my feet. The interior was full of guests, all talking at once. I stripped off my coat and walked behind the desk, patting her arm as I stowed my bag under the counter.

"What do I need to do?"

"You're an angel. We're offering everyone a free weekend, all-inclusive. Mr. Marsburg signed off on it. We just need to print out their vouchers, but I'm struggling. It just won't print!"

"Okay. I'll get the printer going and then I'll jump in to help with this line. You've got this, Wendy."

Her flushed face broke into a smile, and she nodded sharply. I turned to the computer and scanned the screen, looking for the printer icon. Aha! A printer jam. I dropped to my knees and popped open the hatch. A few minutes later, the vouchers began spitting out of the machine. I grabbed a handful and passed them to Wendy before taking the spot next to her.

"Next?"

An older couple approached, their faces painted with an identical expression. These were two people who lived on gossip. Oh boy.

"Yes, I'm Edward, and this is Clara. What's going on here?"

"I'm afraid I don't have the specifics, but there was an incident that occurred earlier. No one is in danger, but we're offering a free weekend stay to all our guests as an apology for any inconvenience you might have suffered," I said, marveling as the words fell out of my mouth.

Wendy elbowed me in the side while whispering.

"Good one. I'm going to steal that."

"I should've known we'd get the official line," Edward grumbled, slapping the counter lightly. "I can't blame you. We'll take the voucher."

His wife's face twisted as she realized they wouldn't get much out of me, but they weren't so disappointed they'd give up their free stay. I asked for their name and current room number, jotted down the information on the voucher and handed it back to him. He looked it over before nodding and shuffling off.

A man stepped into his place and I began the same routine. By the time the lobby was empty, my mind was numb and my voice was going craggy. Wendy leaned against the counter and heaved an enormous sigh.

"Thanks for saving my bacon, kiddo. I don't think I've ever had to deal with anything like this before."

I glanced around to confirm we were alone and leaned in close.

"Do you know what happened? Charlie said it was the couple in room 413."

Wendy ran her hand through her hair and looked over her shoulder.

"It was the wife. Mr. Marsburg and Penny know more than I do. I walked into this mess. Mr. Marsburg loaded up the file and helped, but he got called away by someone official looking and I haven't seen him since. What a morning."

"The wife?"

She held up her hand and stood back up.

"That's what I heard. It might be wrong. Don't quote me. But if you ask me, it was the husband who did it. It always is in the shows, isn't it?"

I tapped my finger on my lip. She had a point, but something felt off. I couldn't put my finger on it, but I had little to go on. I grabbed my bag and smiled at Wendy.

"Well, let me know if you hear anything else. I'm going to head to my office, but holler if you get swarmed again."

"My angel Eden. Hey, that's funny. Garden of Eden and all that."

I grinned and headed down the hall, my footsteps pausing at Mr. Marsburg's door. It was propped open, and the lights were off. I kept going and walked into my office, shutting the door behind me and leaning on it. I was finally alone.

It felt like a wave of emotion as everything that happened in the last twenty-four hours crashed on top of me. Finding Jasper. Talking to Hannah and Anastasia. Conversing with a cat. Coming back to the resort to a potential murder. My mind still didn't want to wrap itself around the last part. Or to be honest, most of it.

I sank into my desk chair and swiveled around, kicking my feet like a kid. I was pretty vertically challenged, and my only option if I wanted to reach my keyboard was to lift the chair up so high my feet wouldn't touch the ground.

Once my computer was powered up, I attempted to go through the PR courses I'd started the day before, but my brain refused to focus. After failing a pop quiz twice, I closed my browser window and swiveled around again.

Here I was, living my dream. I was due to start my college courses soon, and already working at what could honestly be my dream job. I knew it was too soon to tell, but I was already fitting in. I sucked in a breath as more pieces of the puzzle fell into place. Was it meant to be?

Is that why Hannah recommended me for this job? From what I could glean from our call last night, she could talk to cats as well. So could Anastasia. She already knew the names of the clowder cats before I even showed up. What was really going on here? Did they know I shared the same ability? How common was it, anyway?

I pulled up a new browser window and typed in 'people who talk to cats,' feeling silly and half dreading the results. Thousands of answers came back to my question, but after spending half an hour sorting through them, I didn't know what to think. I pushed back from my desk and pulled a notepad out of my top drawer. Maybe a list would help me organize my mind.

I tapped the end of my pen on the desk for a few seconds before scribbling furiously. Once I was halfway through the sheet, I stopped and read through it.

Point one. Hannah, Anastasia, and I all shared what appeared to be a unique ability to understand cats. Point two. Even though this was firmly in the hard to believe category, I had enough proof to accept it. At least for now. The odds of the three of us sharing a delusion were small. Too many facts checked out.

That sorted, I moved onto point three. Had a murder taken place at the resort? My gut instinct said yes. From what Wendy inferred, the husband was believed to have killed his wife. But I'd seen the man threaten Penny. Was that proof he was violent? Or was the unlikeable Penny somehow involved? Why had he come here, a place full of people, to kill his wife? A pair of blue eyes over a freckled nose floated through my brain. What did Ethan Rhodes think?

That was a question I couldn't answer, but the first few I could tackle. I swung around and hopped out of my chair. The best place to look for my answers wasn't here. It was in Trevor's office. I headed down the hall and turned right, glancing at the name plates until I found the one with Trevor's name. I rapped on the door and twisted my fingers together, something I hadn't done since I was a little girl..

"Come on in."

Hearing Trevor's voice boom through the door shook me out of my memories and I walked in, surprised at how dark the room was.

"Trevor?"

"Back here, behind the monitors."

Trevor's face was drawn and his smile was shaky.

"Eden. It's good to see you. How are you fitting in?"

"Just fine. Everyone here is so nice. Hey, I'm sorry to bother you, but do you have a second?"

He closed something on his main screen and folded his hands in front of him.

"Sure. Oh, how's your car?"

I blinked, realizing I'd completely forgotten about the hunk of junk.

"Oh. I should ask Wendy if the garage called. I totally spaced it off."

Trevor grimaced and rubbed his bearded cheeks.

"Yeah. This is the second time something like this has happened here, but I can't say I'm any more prepared. I've been reviewing footage all morning, but I've come up with nothing. Detective Rhodes was in here earlier, but he couldn't find anything, either."

I leaned forward.

"Do you have cameras in the halls?"

"We do, but only by the elevators. We've been trying to add more, but it's a delicate balance with guest security, versus making them feel like they're in a police state."

"How about the stairwell?"

"We went through that footage, too. The fourth floor was quiet after ten. Nothing showed up between that time and when the maid started screaming. It's frustrating."

He hung his head and rubbed the back of his neck.

"It's not your fault, Trevor," I said, reaching across the desk to pat his hand. "You've down what you can. It must be like Wendy said. The husband must have killed his wife in his room."

"You haven't heard, have you?"

"What?"

"The husband got called away on a business matter right after they checked in. The wife was here alone."

I reared my head back.

"No way! How did she end up?"

"Dead? No one knows. I was sitting here while Ethan made the call to notify him of his wife's death. It was awful. He had me check the footage to confirm the alibi. He definitely left the resort and hasn't returned. We've got all that on tape. No one entered the room or left it until Jemma showed up. It's the craziest thing."

I thought for a second before something clicked.

"Why was Jemma there so early? Did they request something special? I haven't stayed in many hotels, but from the estate where I worked, typically, housekeeping didn't bother going into any rooms until after eleven."

"I don't know," Trevor said, throwing his hands wide. "Jemma says she received a message from Penny that Room 413 was requesting fresh towels. She's the only one on the morning shift, so she headed right there."

"Towels?"

"Yeah. And from what Detective Rhodes said, the early news from the coroner was that the time of death was well before six-thirty."

"How bizarre. It's a locked room mystery?"

"A what now?"

"You know. From mystery novels. One person in a room, they end up dead, and it's up to the sleuth to figure out who killed them."

"Oh. I see. Well, that's what Detective Rhodes is for, I guess. I've done everything I can and supplied him with all the footage. I've gone through it all twice now and I have seen nothing."

I drummed my fingers on his desk, debating on my next move.

"Could you share it with me? I know you've got Josh on your team, but sometimes a fresh set of eyes is useful."

"Sure. I'll turn on security access for you and you can go right in through our system. I appreciate it."

I stood and held my hand out over his desk. His bear-like mitt enveloped my hand.

"It's the least I can do. You've been so helpful."

He shrugged and stood, towering over me.

"I may as well take a coffee break. Do you want to join me?"

"No thanks. I'm going to get back to work."

"Hey, on a day like today, it's okay to slack a little. I'll get your access set up when I get back, okay?"

I nodded and followed him out of his office and turned off at mine. I thought about sitting in my chair and loading up a PR course again, but changed my mind. I'd told Jasper I'd go see the clowder and now was as good a time as any. It was probably best to do it earlier in the day, so I didn't get caught conversing with a group of cats. I pulled on my coat and headed back through the lobby. Wendy had a small line at the desk, but she shot me a thumbs up as I walked by. Asking about my car was going to wait.

I went through the massive doors and took a left, heading towards the forest. I couldn't wait to talk to the clowder. Even though the brown cat was intimidating, she looked interesting.

# Chapter Twelve

The walk to the forest felt longer than it had the night before, and I jumped at every sound. Was it more than just being on my own instead of having Luke with me? I wasn't sure, but my nerves felt like they were close to the breaking point by the time I made it to the trees.

I paused and took a deep breath, watching as it came out in a puff of fog. I shoved my hands in my pockets and wished I'd brought my gloves. Slowly, I turned in a circle, hoping to get my bearings. I was pretty sure I'd followed nearly the same path Luke had led me on, but nothing looked familiar in the bright light of day.

Well, standing here wouldn't help me find the cats. I walked forward and practiced what I was going to say to the cats when I found them. It seemed silly at first, but by the time I was surrounded by trees, I felt a lot more confident.

"You came back."

I'm not ashamed to admit I let out a squawk that made birds take flight. I'll also admit to nearly jumping out of my skin before I turned around and spotted the brown cat I'd seen the night before. Even though she wasn't surrounded by other cats this time, she was still awe-inspiring. There was just something about her.

"Fig? Is that right?"

She nodded her head once, never taking her eyes off of me.

"That is correct."

"Wow," I said, half to myself.

Her eyes closed briefly as she straightened.

"You are alone. I was hoping..."

"He's okay," I said, cutting her off. "Jasper is alive and healthy. Well, that might be stretching it a little. I took him to the vet, though, and they said he was half-starved and dehydrated. They gave him an I.V. and put him on a special diet. I think he's going to be all right."

Her shoulders slumped and a look of relief blazed briefly in her eyes. She nodded sharply.

"That is good. He can recover here. We'll take care of him. I knew he wasn't eating enough, but that stubborn old codger thought he could fool me. Thank you for taking care of him."

I held up my hand and risked taking a step closer to the beautiful brown cat. I'd never seen a cat with a coat like hers. Her rich brown fur looked like it belonged to a mink, not a cat.

"I think he'd be better off with me. At least for a little while. It's so cold, and he's so frail."

She cocked her head to the side and seemed to consider my statement. I felt like I was in the presence of a queen. A queen who wasn't too sure of me. A sudden crashing noise made me squeak, and I whipped my head to the side, spotting a huge black and white cat coming at me like a bowling ball.

"Interloper! Intruder! Run Fig, I'll save you."

Fig let out what sounded remarkably like a snort before shaking her head and holding up a paw.

"Ollie, that's enough. This human means no harm."

She gave me a look that suggested I'd better not mean them harm or I'd come to a quick end. She may have been less than ten pounds, but I swallowed hard and tried to smile. Something about his name sounded familiar. It took me a second before I realized it. I'd heard the name as I was leaving Anastasia's store. It had to have been Callie who'd made the request.

"Your name is Ollie? Callie said to tell you hi."

The look the pudgy cat gave me would've made me laugh in normal circumstances, but this was anything but. His green eyes goggled at me.

"You've seen Callie? How is she?"

"She's fine. She lives with Anastasia now. I don't know if you know who that is, but she's a very nice..."

"We know her. This is good. Callie wasn't meant for this life," Fig said, while Ollie pranced around, humming to himself. "Ollie. Enough."

"Oh, come on, Fig. Unbend a little. We've just had news about the whippersnapper. Unless. Oh my... Don't tell me..."

"He lives."

Ollie let out a dramatic sigh and flopped onto the forest floor.

"Oooph. I thought I put my paw in it there for a second. Well, that's great news! Where is he? We should have a celebration!"

Something about this overweight tuxedo cat spoke right to my heart. He was obviously wild, but he was a natural goofball. From the look on Fig's face, she didn't share my opinion.

"The human will keep him until he recovers. I have agreed to allow this to happen."

Yep. She was definitely a queen. She'd keep the clowder running smoothly in Jasper's absence.

Ollie hopped up and dashed off, hollering over his shoulder.

"I'll let everyone know. Bye, human!"

I glanced at Fig. Her eyes, so yellow against her fur, narrowed. I cut it out and cleared my throat.

"May I see the other cats? I'd like to meet them. Jasper wanted me to check on everyone."

"You can tell him everything is fine and we are all well. The extra food Luke brought was very useful last night."

I rubbed my hands together.

"Okay. Well, maybe next time. Hey, did you hear anything about the murder at the resort? Something happened at the resort early this morning. I was thinking maybe you or one of the other cats might have seen something. I know you were by my cabin the other night."

Fig stretched, the tips of her ears pointing forwards and wrapped her tail tightly around her flanks.

"We don't involve ourselves in human business. We're grateful to Luke and yourself, but our gratitude doesn't extend towards involving ourselves in whatever goes on in that place. Ollie went against orders the last time he got involved and one of our clowder ended up leaving. I won't let that happen again."

"But you said it was good Callie left. She misses you, though. I can tell."

Her imperious posture relaxed for a second and I knew that the irrepressible Callie had touched this cat's heart, much like she'd touched my own.

"That was then, and this is now," she said, straightening again. "As soon as Jasper is well, bring him here. He'll find his way home from the treeline."

She stalked off, tail waving, and I stood there for a second, flummoxed. This hadn't gone the way I'd thought it would. I hadn't expected Fig to be so unfriendly. The wind whipped through the trees in a moan, and I rubbed my hands together.

It was time to head back. I picked my way through the brush as my mind raced. Maybe they just needed to get to know me. I'd be back with Luke to deliver their food. A plan formed as I neared the dining hall.

Fig mentioned Ollie getting involved before. I was pretty sure that was the investigation Hannah mentioned. If I could get him apart from the others, maybe he'd be willing to help. I had a feeling I knew the way to that cat's heart. I smiled as I walked back to my cabin. Jasper might have some ideas, too.

I opened the door and found Jasper sitting up in his tub, fussing with the scarf I'd folded up inside. I rushed over to help.

"Are you uncomfortable? I'm so sorry. This tub is too small. I need to go to town and get you a proper bed, don't I? Oh shoot, I don't have my car. Dang it. I need to talk to Wendy and see what's going on with that."

"I'm fine. It's just rumpled a little and my leg..."

"You're not fine. You need more room. Are you feeling stronger? I could put you on the bed and you could stretch out."

His ears perked, and I smiled before gently picking him up and carrying him across the small room. I pulled back the corner of the comforter and put him down on the mattress. He let out a sigh as he nestled into the cushy surface.

"This isn't half bad. How was everyone?"

"How was who?"

"Fig. I think I catch a hint of Ollie, too," he said, sniffing my sleeve.

"How can you? That's incredible. I didn't touch either cat."

"I'd know their scents anywhere. Well, how were they?"

I sat next to Jasper and stroked his head while I filled him in on my brief visit with Fig. He nodded as I came to the part about the clowder not getting involved with the resort.

"I know Fig can appear harsh, but she's a good leader. Tough, but fair. I've taught her everything I know. She'll be perfect when my time comes."

My hand stilled. I didn't want to think about that. Not one bit.

"Jasper..."

"Hush. I've lived a long life. I thought I was done, but apparently, I'm still here. Since I have you to thank for that, I'll help you with your investigation. You are going to investigate, aren't you?"

I nodded and tapped on my lip. I still had a few days before my classes started, and before I needed to really get into the swing at my new job. I had some extra time on my hands. Even though Detective Rhodes seemed very capable, I wouldn't mind helping. I mean, yeah, he hadn't asked me to, but I worked here, right? I had a vested interest in helping catch a killer.

"I am. But you didn't see what happened, and neither did I. How can we figure it out?"

"I might be an old feral cat, but I've been around enough humans to understand the way they work. Now, tell me what you've learned so far."

I settled back into the mattress and repeated everything I'd found out. He was an excellent listener and by the time I was done, I was more sure than ever I wanted to solve this case.

"Oh! Let's look at the security footage together. I bet Trevor's given me access."

I hopped up and grabbed my new laptop from my bag. Within a few minutes, I'd downloaded the resort's software and logged in. Trevor hadn't forgotten me. I logged into the security portal and watched as the video streams loaded.

Jasper leaned close as I went through each video, trying to figure out how everything worked.

"This is something else," he said, while I clicked buttons. "Imagine if cats had access to this kind of technology? We'd rule the world."

I didn't doubt it. From what little I'd seen of the inner lives of cats, humans had been selling them seriously short. I found the footage from the hallway of the fourth floor and hit play.

"Okay, this is the hallway from the elevator. Trevor said the husband left shortly after they checked in. That was right before I ate dinner last night. Let's check the footage."

I hit the fast-forward button and quickly stopped it once it hit the right time frame. Sure enough, there was Brad Youngstown, walking to the elevator, alone. He didn't look happy. The force he used to press the button could've broken it. I sped up the footage and saw nothing until a girl pushed a cart out of the elevator. That had to be Jemma.

I pushed the laptop off my lap and grabbed the end of my braid, twirling it around.

"Huh. So, no one was seen in that hallway for that long. The husband's alibi holds up."

"Isn't that a little strange? I know little of hotels, though," Jasper said, stretching a little before hunkering back down into his spot.

His eyes were heavy, and I closed the laptop. He needed rest.

"I think it's strange. But the camera doesn't lie."

Jasper's eyes closed before flaring open.

"But what about what the camera doesn't see?"

"What do you mean?"

"I mean, there has to be more than one way into the rooms. I would start there."

I nodded and eased off the bed, grabbing the laptop.

"Thanks, Jasper. Get some rest. I've got to go back to work. I'll be back after dinner. I'll bring you back a treat."

He let out a rusty purr and closed his eyes again. I stowed my laptop and checked his water and food bowls before tiptoeing back outside. I needed to do a little recon around the grounds of the resort. Jasper was right. There had to be more ways to access the rooms.

# Chapter Thirteen

Luckily, the sidewalk that encircled the main resort building had been cleared off. My socks were still a little damp from my journey into the forest and I'd forgotten to change them. As I walked, I realized I had taken much time to familiarize myself with the resort since I started. I snorted and kept walking, looking up at the side of the building. It was all stuccoed over, and from my view-point, there wasn't an easy way for anyone to make it to the fourth floor, at least from the outside.

So much for that theory. I shuffled into the lobby and spotted Wendy leaning against the counter, drinking out of a cup. She gave me a friendly wave as I walked up.

"Hey. Thanks again for bailing me out."

"No worries. Before I forget, has the garage called about my car?"

She slapped her hand to her forehead and let out a groan.

"I totally forgot to tell you. They called right when I got in, but with everything that happened... I'm so sorry."

"It's fine, Wendy. I appreciate you taking the message. What did they say?"

"Something about the doohickey being busted. I'm terrible with car lingo," she said, shuffling papers around under the desk. "Here it is! You've got just enough time to call them back. I think they're open until five."

She passed me the resort phone, and I punched in the number. I'd never really dealt with a mechanic before and felt completely out of my depth as a harsh voice barked through the line.

"Sullivans."

"Um. Hi. This is Eden Brooks. I work up at the Valewood Resort and I'm returning your call. I think my car is in there?"

I winced as my words came tumbling out. Why did I have to be so awkward?

"One sec, lemme ask Jim."

In the background, I could hear what was a power tool or the scream of a soul being tortured. I hoped it was a power tool.

"Yello. This is Jim."

"Hi, Jim. This is Eden Brooks. I'm calling about my car."

There! I nailed it. For once.

"Oh right. You've got that old Chevy, right?"

"That's me. What's wrong with it?"

"Well, besides the fact I think that cars older than you are, not much. It needs a new alternator, and one of your belts was about to break. I can take care of everything and make sure all your fluids are topped off for about five hundred bucks."

Wendy, who'd been leaning in the entire time Jim was speaking, shot me two thumbs up. Good thing. I didn't know if that was a fair price, but it sure seemed like it.

"Great! Let's do it," I said. "When should it be done?"

"I can fit it in tonight before I go home. You can pick it up tomorrow morning at eight, okay?"

"Thanks, Jim. See you then!"

I handed the phone back to Wendy, grinning from ear to ear. I was getting my wheels back. While I was in town, I'd try to find a pet store and pick up a few things for Jasper. Reality hit when I realized I didn't have a way to get to the garage.

"I'll drop you off, honey. My shift starts at nine, so that will be perfect."

"You're the best. Hey, while I've got you here. I was wondering... are there any ways to get into a room here without going through the main door?"

Wendy blinked at my conversation shift, but she caught up quickly.

"Well, that depends. Some of the rooms have connecting doors. Some don't. Otherwise, the only way into a room is through a window, and that only works on the first floor. Or if you've got an enormous ladder."

I mentally played with the ladder theory before dismissing it. The odds of someone carrying a tall ladder around the resort and not being noticed were small.

"Sweet. Can you tell which rooms have connecting doors?"

Wendy cocked her head to the side and narrowed her eyes.

"You want to know about room 413, don't you? What have you heard?"

She leaned across the desk, eyes bright, while I filled her in on what I'd learned from Trevor. She slapped her hand on the desk and looked around.

"Well, I can't give you the key for that room, but I can give you 415 and 411 if you want to check it out. No one's using those rooms right now."

She tapped away on the computer and grabbed two blank keys.

"Wait. Was anyone in those rooms last night?"

She paused, hovering her hand above the key reader. Her eyes focused on a point behind my shoulder, and she nodded slowly.

"411 was empty, but there was someone in 415. Why? Do you think they did it?"

"Who knows? But it might be the best lead we've got."

Excitement thrummed through my veins and I could hardly contain myself as Wendy got the keys ready. She slid them across the desk and leaned closer.

"I'd go with you, but I've got to man the desk. If Penny caught me away from here, she'd probably get me fired. Be careful though. If you're not back in ten minutes, I'm calling Trevor."

"He'll see me through the camera feed," I said, sliding the keys into my back pocket. "I'll be back in a few."

I headed for the elevators and pushed the button once, and then a few more times for good measure. It felt like an eternity before it dinged. I hustled inside and hit the button for the fourth floor, and then the close door button.

I paced back and forth as the elevator made its way up. Maybe it would've been faster to take the stairs. I spotted myself in the polished doors and blinked, horrified. My beanie was listing to one side, and some hair had frizzled out of my fishtail braid. I crammed my hat back on my head, hiding the worst of it.

The doors slid open, and I glanced at the signs before heading left. I pulled out the keys and move to try 415 first. The door to 413 was closed, but I gave it a wide berth anyway as I passed. I slid the key into the reader of 415 and waited for the light to turn green, giving the heavy door a push to get inside.

The room was spotless and chilly. I rubbed my hands together as I walked through the space, searching for a door. I hadn't been in many hotel rooms, but this one seemed super nice. I gasped as I spotted a door, only to realize it was on the wrong side of the room. I turned in a circle, taking in the layout, before leaving. If that door was on the left side of the room, that meant room 411 was the one I wanted.

I hustled over to that room and repeated the process to get inside. I raced in and pumped my fist when I spotted the door. This was it. I cracked the case wide open. I put my hand on the door handle and turned it, just to see what would happen. It turned, and I paused.

Did I want to see what was on the other side? From Charlie's report, Jemma had seen a ton of blood. I didn't need to see that. I put my hand on the door and eased it back into place, jumping when a voice rang out.

"Who's there? Step away from the door."

The commanding voice made my heart leap into my chest and I stammered out a quick reply.

"Don't shoot! I'm not a killer."

I closed my eyes and put my hands in the air, even though I was alone in the room. The door flung open, and I met a familiar pair of blue eyes. Right now, they weren't giving out glacier lake vibes. Nope, they were more like a lake of furious lava. Well, if lava could be blue. Why was I thinking about his eyes?

"Eden. It's you. What are you doing up here?"

"What are you doing here?"

"I asked you first," he said, holstering his weapon.

I couldn't take my eyes off the gun as I licked my lips. My curiosity had almost landed me in some serious hot water.

"Sorry! I was talking to Wendy about how someone could have gotten into this room and she mentioned connecting doors. I didn't think anyone was in there. The door was shut when I checked out Room 415."

Ethan's eyes softened, and he put his hands on his hips.

"I see. Doing a little amateur sleuthing? I see you take after your friend, Hannah."

I licked my lips again.

"Something like that. I wasn't trying to muck up your investigation. Anyway, there wasn't anyone staying in this room last night, anyway. That's why I started with the other room."

"No, good work. I already had Trevor check the logs, but you've got good instincts."

I felt ridiculously proud as I straightened up to my full height. I barely came to the top of Ethan's shoulder. Why did I notice that?

"Thanks. I really thought I'd cracked the case wide open, but I guess not. How's your investigation going?"

He leaned back against the wall and crossed his arms over his chest. He was slim but well muscled. Distractingly so.

"I'm at a stand-still. The crime scene techs released the room, so I came by to get a feel for the place before calling in the cleaning crew. They're a good team, but everyone's human. I was hoping there was something small they'd missed, but I don't think so."

I stared at the door he'd propped open, hoping I wouldn't see any blood on the floor. I wasn't ready for that.

"Did the husband's alibi check out? I met them briefly yesterday. He seemed like he'd be a nice man when he wasn't angry."

"He was angry?"

Ethan's eyes lit and he leaned in closer. I took a quick breath and inhaled a burst of cinnamon and a citrus scent I couldn't quite define. I nodded.

"He was. He had words with Penny. She's the head of the housekeeping staff. I guess she was manning the desk when they made their reservation. He said something about having a suite since they were celebrating their anniversary. He was mad they didn't get one. Anyway, he kinda sorta threatened her."

Ethan grabbed my arm, and I winced, stepping back so fast I bonked my head on the wall.

He let me go and held up both hands.

"Eden. I'm sorry. I didn't mean to scare you. I should've known better than to grab you like that. I'm so sorry."

"What do you mean?"

He ran a hand through his hair and looked down.

"I ran your name and talked to Ben Walsh about the case you were involved in. I apologize."

"Are you apologizing for grabbing me or for looking me up behind my back?"

My heart skittered as I stepped away from Ethan. I felt strange, like I'd caught him gossiping about me. Even though I trusted Ben, and I knew a lot of the details about the case were public record, it still felt invasive.

"I have to run everyone at the resort, Eden. You've got to understand that. This is an active murder investigation. I have to follow every avenue."

While my mind knew he was completely within his rights to do that, my heart refused to budge. I pivoted and took another step away from him.

"I see. Anyway. The husband, Brad, pointed at Penny and said he wouldn't forget this and she'd wish she hadn't messed with him. It seemed a little excessive, but Penny had promised them a suite, and well, Penny's not the nicest person."

Ethan's face grew taut, and he rubbed his chin.

"That's the first hint of a motive I've had so far. Thanks, Eden. Again, I'm sorry. I didn't mean to hurt you. What I read and what I learned from Ben goes no further."

His eyes were sincere and my heart softened. A little. There was still a twinge that wasn't going away. My past wasn't something I enjoyed talking about, but I still preferred to be the one to decide to tell someone about it. I wrapped my arms around my stomach and nodded.

"I understand. I'd better go. I still need to get some work done."

I turned on my heel and marched out of the room. Ethan was silent, and I let the heavy door into the hall bang loudly as I left.

I walked towards the elevator, still gripping my middle. I'd told him I needed to work, but all I wanted to do was go back to my cabin, turn off the lights, and be alone. I spotted the stairwell and took that route instead. As I stumbled down the steps, I remembered Wendy saying she'd send in the troops if I wasn't back by a certain time. I grabbed my phone and fired off a quick text to her. I wasn't in the mood to see anyone face to face. Not now.

# Chapter Fourteen

J asper was still cuddled in bed when I returned to my room. The short walk through the snow had done little to improve my mood, but seeing him when I flipped on the light helped. He squinted his golden eyes in my direction before stretching out a leg and settling his head back down onto the comforter.

"A guy could get used to comforts like this," he said, his voice soft. "Even though it's temporary, I may as well enjoy it while I can."

I tossed my bag down, took off my beanie, and shrugged out of my coat, desperate to keep tears from flowing down my face. Jasper cracked an eye open again and looked at me.

"What's wrong?"

"Nothing," I said, hanging up my things by the door. "Did you get anything to eat while I was gone?"

I heard a soft thump followed by a sound that could only be described as a rusty chirp. I slowly turned and found Jasper making his way across the floor. His strides were slow, but he didn't seem to be in any pain. I held my breath as he approached and sat in front of me.

"I haven't. What do you have? And I'm not buying that whole nothing is wrong thing. I can feel your sadness."

I turned back to the counter, unable to meet his eyes. Instead, I busied myself dishing up some of the special canned food the vet recommended. I slid it down in front of him and tried to smile.

"This is supposed to be good for you," I said. "It says it's turkey flavored."

Jasper took a delicate sniff before staring up at me, his expressive eyes dubious.

"Turkey, huh? I've had wild turkey before, and I'm telling you it smells nothing like this."

"Well, it's full of vitamins and nutrients. Maybe that's what you're smelling."

He took a small bite and licked his chops.

"It'll do. Now, tell me what's bothering you."

He methodically ate his food while I took a deep breath and tried to find my words. As usual, they all came spilling out until I was spent, tears running down my cheeks.

Jasper blinked slowly at me before wiping his face with a paw. I wiped my cheeks, suddenly embarrassed.

"I'm sorry. I babble when I'm upset. And tired. And stressed."

He stopped bathing for a second and shook his grizzled head.

"Never apologize for feeling the way you do. It's natural to be upset. You've dealt with a lot in your life. Now, let's go sit in that chair over there and unpack it all."

It took a second to sink in. Did he want me to pick him up and cuddle him? This wild cat who just days ago had been firmly entrenched in clowder life?

He rolled his golden eyes and started walking stiffly towards the chair. I guess that meant yes, that's exactly what he wanted. Who was I to argue? I followed, took a seat and gently picked him up, scared I'd hurt him somehow.

"I'm not made of glass. I'll admit I've felt better, but you don't have to treat me like I'm going to fall apart. Unless the vet told you something I didn't hear."

He settled into my lap, folding his legs until he was a Jasper sized loaf. His familiar rusty purr started up, and I felt myself relax a smidge.

"Never fails. You start the old engine and humans melt. Do you want to start with the detective or the mystery?"

"The mystery," I said, unwilling to even think about Ethan right now.

"Sounds good to me. I'm not one for mushy stuff. Okay, so there wasn't anyone staying in Room 411, correct?"

"That's right. Wendy said it was empty."

"And no one was seen entering the room the victim was in after the husband left?"

"Right. The hallway was empty of any other guests."

"So, who would have access to the rooms?"

I paused, my hand hovering over his head as my gears started turning.

"I guess the housekeeping staff would have to have some sort of main key that works in all the rooms."

"And a member of that staff got into a verbal altercation with the victim's husband?"

"You think Penny killed her?"

Jasper shifted his weight around and laid down his head.

"I'm saying it's possible."

"Wendy said that Penny always seemed to have an issue with happy couples. But to kill someone? That seems like an overreaction. I mean, Brad pointed his finger into her chest and threaten her, but to jump to murdering his wife..."

"One thing I've learned on all my trips around the sun is never to put anything past a human. There's no rhyme or reason to what they're capable of. Especially if their hearts are involved."

There was a distinct note in his voice as he finished. I stroked his head again, curious.

"How did you end up in the wild, anyway? You mentioned someone cared for you once. What happened to her? Would you like me to find her?"

Jasper shook his head slightly.

"You don't want to talk about your detective and I don't want to talk about the human. Let's leave it at that."

His purrs petered out, and I bit my lip.

"I'm sorry, Jasper. I didn't mean to say the wrong thing."

"You didn't, kiddo. Some day, I might tell you my story, but not tonight. Besides, it sounds to me like you've got a murderer to catch. That takes importance."

He was right. My heart needed to mind its own business and stop thinking about Ethan Rhodes. My brain was the one who should be on center stage.

"Okay. So, what should I do next?"

"What would the character in your favorite book do?"

"She'd learn everything she could about the suspect and then figure out a way to make it all come together."

"Then that's what you need to do. Me? I think I'm going to catch up on a little sleep."

I stood carefully, holding my arms around him. I placed Jasper back on the bed and grabbed my laptop before climbing up next to him. His whiskers quirked as I scooted closer to him.

"So first, I need to find Penny's last name. I bet I can get that through the portal," I said, half to myself, half to Jasper.

It took me a few minutes to log in and surf through all the areas until I found the staff logs. There! Penny Abrams. I briefly wondered if Penny was short for Penelope, and searched for both names. I flipped over to my browser and typed in her name. I wasn't sure what I was looking for, but landing on a giant red flag that pointed to her as a murderer would be nice.

I knew it wouldn't be that easy, but a girl could hope, right? I spent the next hour sifting through so much information it felt like my eyes were going to cross. I'd come up empty. Zilch, nothing, nada. No social media accounts, no old news articles. It was as if she didn't exist.

Frustrated, I closed my laptop and rested my head on my knees. My stomach rumbled. But the thought of facing everyone in the dining hall did not appeal. I'd missed meals before and it wouldn't kill me to miss another. Wait! I'd stowed away half of a sandwich in the fridge.. My stomach rumbled, this time in anticipation.

I got up and peeked into the fridge. Sure enough, there it was! I grabbed it, unwrapped the plastic film, and put about half of it in my mouth. Still good. I chewed happily and bounced over to the kitchen to grab a glass of water. I leaned back against the counter and finished my meal, feeling better with every bite. I dusted my hands off and tried to figure out my next move.

Obviously, Ethan Rhodes would have more resources than I did to learn more about Penny and her background, but there was no way I was going to reach out to him. At least, not right away. Now that I'd calmed down, I knew what he'd done was standard, and it wasn't his fault he'd come across something I'd rather he hadn't.

Still. I didn't feel like talking to him. Or thinking about him. Even though that seemed increasingly difficult. I tossed the plastic wrap into the recycling bin and paced around the cabin. I felt stuck. I needed better resources, but I didn't know any cops. My eyes flew open as I realized there was someone who could help. Someone who was close to a cop and also was one of the best investigative journalists in the state. I grabbed my phone, sat back on the bed, and dialed Hannah's number.

She picked up on the first ring, startling me.

"Eden! I'm so glad you called. I've been worried sick about you. How is..."

"Oh! You must mean the murder that happened. No, I'm fine. I should've known you would've heard about it," I said, jumping over her words.

"Murder? No. I meant what happened with you and Jasper last night. There was a murder?"

"You must not have talked to Ben yet," I said, settling back against the bed. "Ethan said he talked to him today."

"He's due home any minute. What happened? How's Jasper? And how's Ethan?"

I skipped my thoughts on Ethan and jumped right into the heart of the subject.

"A guest was killed here today. It's the strangest thing. I have a suspect, but I can't find anything about her. I was wondering if..."

"I'd love to help! I'm sorry to hear about someone dying, though. Are you sure you're okay? I thought I was sending you to a good place, but now I feel terrible."

"It's not your fault, Hannah. This is the best job I think I've ever had. The people, well, most of them, are so nice. And then you've got the clowder and Jasper. He's going to be okay. I took him to the vet this morning. When we got back, there were police cars everywhere."

"Okay, let's start at the beginning. I'm already confused."

I took a deep breath.

"Sorry, I'm all scrambled. Okay, here's what happened after we got off the phone. I have some questions about that call last night, but they can wait."

I launched into my story and did my best not to leave anything out. Once I was done, I heard a delicate voice come on the line.

"Hi Eden. This is Razzy. Can you describe Penny's face when the man threatened her?"

I blinked, surprised at her question.

"Um. You know what, she didn't look scared. If someone was threatening me, I think I'd be all flustered. She looked... happy?"

"Interesting. Please say hello to Jasper for me. Sorry, mama. You can have the phone back."

A giggle burbled out of my mouth before I could contain it. Who would have thought I'd ever be able to talk to cats? Wonder and delight warred in my chest as I realized the potential of my new ability. I'd focused on just getting through the moments I hadn't even considered the bigger picture.

"Eden? Are you there?"

"I'm here, Hannah. Just lost in thought. I never would've imagined I could hear them. Razzy sounds just as sweet as she looks."

"She does, doesn't she? Smart as a whip, too. Okay, here's what we'll do. I'll run Penny's name through my database. Once Ben gets home, I'll see if he can help, too. In the meantime, don't approach Penny on your own. We have to assume she's dangerous. It's one thing to do a little legwork, but this is Ethan's case, and you need to stay safe."

I heard Razzy in the background as she piped up.

"But mama, have you ever taken that advice?"

I smothered a laugh as Hannah sputtered. Just talking to her brought back the light that had gone out when I'd realized what Ethan had done. I felt better than I had in days. She came back on the line.

"Razzy has a good point. And it's nearly gotten me killed, so please do nothing rash. I'm so glad to hear about Jasper. I'd love to talk with him."

I glanced down and saw the older cat was still out cold, sides rising and falling rhythmically.

"He's still sleeping, but maybe tomorrow. So, tell me all about how you found out you could talk to cats. I'm dying to know."

"It's a long story."

"I've got time."

We spent the next hour talking as Hannah related her exploits with her amazing felines. Now that I knew the truth, so many things about her and her cats made sense. It was amazing, and wonderful, and there were flashes where I wasn't sure if I was awake or dreaming, but I couldn't deny what had taken place.

"Ben's home. I've got to go. I'll call you in the morning with what I find out. Good night, Eden. Give Jasper a kiss from all of us."

Hannah ended the call, and I leaned back into my pillow. I needed to get changed to go to bed, but I felt so invigorated, I couldn't imagine sleeping. I smiled to myself as I reached for the book next to the bed. Maybe I'd be the one solving a murder mystery. With Hannah's help, it felt like anything was possible.

# Chapter Fifteen

When I woke up the next morning, Ethan Rhodes was the furthest thing from my mind. He hadn't bothered my dreams in the slightest. Maybe if I said that to myself enough times, I'd actually believe it. I washed my face and looked at myself in the mirror, pointing my finger at my reflection.

"Get it together. You have enough to think about."

"What was that?"

I stuck my head out of the bathroom door and spotted Jasper sitting on the kitchen counter.

"You got up there all by yourself?"

He picked his head up from his bowl and shot me a look that spoke volumes. Okay, note to self, don't unintentionally insult the cat. Got it.

"What did you say while you were in there?"

"Nothing. It doesn't matter. I'll freshen up your water and scoop the litter. I can't wait to get my car back," I said, bouncing a little. "I'll stop and pick up a few things for you."

Jasper shifted on the counter, unable to meet my eyes.

"You shouldn't. I'll only be here for another day or two. You've already spent enough on me. That vet visit couldn't have been cheap."

I planted a quick kiss on his forehead without thinking about it. I wasn't sure who looked more surprised, but I didn't miss the way Jasper briefly closed his eyes as his whiskers curled.

"It was worth every penny. I'll be back later. Do you want me to leave the television on for you? It's gotta be boring in here by yourself."

If a cat could look flustered, Jasper certainly did. He managed a nod, and I ran over to the bed and grabbed the remote. I wasn't sure what he'd like to watch, so I left it on a local channel.

"I've gotta go meet Wendy. See you later, Jasper."

I waved as I walked outside and ran straight into someone.

"Oof. Remind me to stay out of your way," Charlie said, rubbing her arm. "What's going on?"

I patted her arm awkwardly.

"I'm so sorry. I didn't expect you to be right on the other side of the door."

"Hey, next time I'll whistle or something. Where are you going in such a hurry?"

"Wendy's taking me into town to pick up my car," I said, walking ahead as a thought occurred to me. "Who's manning the desk?"

"I asked Danny to watch it. I was worried about you when I didn't see you last night. I was going to come knock, but your lights were out."

Remorse made my stomach hurt as I slowed my steps.

"I'm sorry, Charlie. Yesterday was... well, it was a rough day. I just needed to decompress by myself."

"No worries," she said, giving me a sunny smile. "Since Danny's at the desk, I'll go into town with you. He won't mind."

She dropped a wink, which made me question just how much Danny would mind stretching out his generosity, but I couldn't deny my new friend. I spotted Wendy as she made her way across the parking lot, waving at us.

"There she is. I'm so excited about getting my car back. Oh, hey, is there a pet store in town?"

"Yep. I'll show you where it is if you tell me what happened yesterday."

I quirked my lips to the side before I answered.

"You know, I could just search it on Google."

"You could, but where's the fun in that? Now spill. I can tell something's up."

"Hang on until we're in the car. I have a feeling Wendy's going to want to know, too."

Charlie skipped ahead, and I marveled at her energy. We were about the same age, but she seemed lighter somehow. Unburdened by life. I heaved a quick sigh and shook my head. Maybe I'd get to that point some day. In the meantime, having a friend like her meant the world to me.

She was briskly chattering away with Wendy by the time I joined them.

"Shotgun!"

I groaned as Charlie stuck her tongue out of me and dashed ahead to the passenger side.

Once we were on our way, Charlie spun around in her seat.

"Okay, spill it."

Wendy met my eyes in the rearview mirror briefly and shot me a reassuring smile. I sorted through my thoughts before deciding to lay it all on them. My suspicions, my encounter with Ethan, everything. I felt wrung out by the time we rolled into town.

"Well, no wonder you holed up in your room and didn't stop by the desk on your way out," Wendy said. "You okay, honey?"

I nodded, tears welling behind my eyes. Everyone was so nice here.

"Well, at least we've decided we don't like that nasty detective," Charlie said. "He overstepped big time."

"Oh, I don't know," I said, looking out the window as we rolled into the service garage. "He's just doing his job."

"Well, he didn't need to be such a butt about it."

Wendy stopped the car and put it in park before turning to face me.

"Are you sure about Penny? I mean, she's as nasty as they come, but I don't know about her murdering someone. Do you think she's dangerous?"

I shrugged and shook my head.

"I don't have any evidence that says she is, but I think it's interesting nothing comes up about her. Hopefully, Hannah will get some intel and get back to me. Speaking of Penny, I haven't seen her. Have you?"

"How exciting," Charlie said, bouncing in her seat. "I feel like a spy. I saw her this morning. She clicked past me in those dang high heels like she always does. I'm not one of her favorite people, so whenever she passes me without speaking, I count myself lucky."

I glanced at the clock on the dash.

"We'd better hurry. I don't want to make you late for work, Wendy. Thanks for the ride."

"Any time. Do you want me to stay to make sure your car starts?"

"No, thank you, though. I think it will be okay. I've got a quick stop to make and then I'll be in. I hope I won't be late."

She waved me off.

"Mr. Marsburg rarely makes it in before ten. I wouldn't worry too much. See you girls later."

Charlie hopped out and banged on the roof of the car before closing the door.

"Let's get your wheels back. Later, Wendy."

Wendy rolled her eyes before pulling out of the space. I stood, looking up at the front entrance, suddenly uncertain.

"Come on," Charlie said. "Let's get you paid up and let's hit the road."

She hauled me in behind her and before I knew it, I'd paid my bill and was holding my keys.

"It's right over there, miss. Are you new in town?" the young man behind the register asked.

I nodded and turned to look in the direction he'd pointed.

There she was, my precious old car that had seen me through so much.

"Hey, I love the color," Charlie said. "Thanks, Frank."

I followed her out of the shop.

"How did you know his name was Frank?" I asked, puffing as I tried to keep up.

"His name tag, silly. Unless, of course, he borrowed that shirt, and in that case, hey, it's not my fault if it's wrong."

I couldn't argue with her logic as I plopped into my familiar driver's seat. She wasn't much, but she was mine, and it felt good to be behind the wheel again. I started the engine and was surprised to hear it purr right to life.

"Okay, you're going to want to turn left as we leave," Charlie said, buckling her seat belt. "It's not much, but they should have what you need."

Fifteen minutes later and several dollars lighter, we were headed back to the resort, the back seat piled high with cat toys, bowls, and anything else I could think of that Jasper might enjoy.

"Do you think Penny did it?" I said, turning down the music.

Charlie paused mid head-bob and looked at me.

"Seriously? I'm not sure. She's awful. I mean seriously awful. But is she murderer awful? I don't know."

"Yeah. I don't know either."

In the bright light of day, my certainty faded. It seemed preposterous. Why would she risk her job and kill someone at the resort? Maybe I needed to go back to the drawing board. I glanced over and noticed Charlie was yawning as we pulled onto the highway leading to the resort.

"I don't know how you work nights," I said, turning down the music a little more.

"Eh, it's not bad. I'm a night owl, anyway. Besides, the night time is less busy, so it works out."

"And the night before last, you didn't hear or see anything weird?"

"Not a peep. If it hadn't been for Jemma screaming her head off, I'd never have known anything happened."

"It's just so strange."

"Tell me about it. There I was, a sitting duck, at the front desk, and a murder happened right above my head. I told Detective Rhodes... Oh, sorry, never mind."

"It's okay, you can talk about him."

"Well, he questioned me briefly, and I told him I thought it was really strange that the woman didn't scream. I mean, if someone came at me with a knife, I'd be yelling my head off."

"Unless she knew her. That, or the murderer, is a trained assassin who could kill silently."

Charlie looked at me and blinked.

"Sorry, I read a lot," I said, stammering.

"No, you're a genius!" Charlie said, sitting up straighter. "If we can prove Penny knew the woman, we'll have the missing link."

I drummed my hands on the steering wheel as my mind went over the pieces. Maybe that was it.

"But they didn't seem like they knew each other when they were checking in. The husband was super angry, but the wife kept saying it was okay."

"Maybe Penny had an affair with Brad and Sherry stole her man. She would've recognized the name when they checked in."

"But wouldn't he have recognized her name? Or her face?"

"Not if she'd had plastic surgery and changed her identity. I'm telling ya, Eden, you're a genius!"

"Whoa. I think we've edged into an alternate reality here."

"Mark my words," Charlie said, stabbing her finger into her palm. "There's a connection. I'd put money on it."

I pulled into the employee lot and turned off the car. I'd only paid attention to our conversation, not even realizing how smoothly it had driven.

"Well, maybe Hannah will have something for me," I said, checking my watch. "She said she'd let me know in the morning."

Charlie yawned and stretched after getting out of the car.

"As soon as you find out, let me know. I don't care if I'm sleeping. And don't confront Penny without me. I want to see her face when they slap the cuffs on her."

I couldn't help but laugh at the expression on Charlie's face. She joined me and walked with me towards the front before peeling off towards the cabins.

"See you later, Eden. Remember, I want to know right away."

I waved as she headed down the path. I walked into the resort and spotted Wendy behind the desk, talking with a guest. I headed down the hall to my office, mind whirring. Even though Charlie's theory had been fanciful, there might be a thread of truth running through it. Until I heard from Hannah, I was stuck with Penny, but that didn't mean I couldn't do more research.

I booted up my work computer and promised myself I'd only spend a few minutes doing research before tackling my online PR courses. I loved this job and didn't want to lose it.

# Chapter Sixteen

At first glance, Brad and Sherry Youngstown seemed like a nice enough couple, visiting a resort for their anniversary. Now that I'd dug into their backgrounds, I was sitting at my computer with my mouth open. I hadn't expected this. A rap on the door caught my attention, and I spotted Trevor standing in the doorway.

"Hey, were you able to access the security footage yesterday? I didn't see you when I came back from lunch."

"I was. Thank you for adding me."

"No problem. Whatcha doing?"

I motioned for him to come in and swiveled the monitor around so he could see it.

"I'm doing some background on the victim. I was totally unprepared for this."

Trevor squinted at the screen and started reading out loud.

"Brad and Sherry Youngstown, seen here leaving the courthouse in North Collinswood, where they escaped penalties on a liability case. The families of the victims are expected to hold a candlelight vigil. What the heck?"

"It gets worse," I said, swiveling my monitor back. "They own a string of apartment complexes in North Collinswood. They were being sued after it was determined a fire that killed twelve people in one of their complexes was caused by their negligence. I've only been searching for ten minutes and I've already found a bunch of awful things. They were slumlords."

Trevor shook his head as he let out a low whistle.

"That's appalling. Those poor family members. Was anything done to help them?"

"I haven't gotten that far. I mean, I feel terrible that she's dead, but wow. This opens up an entirely new suspect pool."

"Speaking of suspects, did you see anything I missed in the footage?"

"I didn't. I'm sorry."

Trevor shrugged his shoulders and headed towards the door, pausing with his hand on the frame.

"Not your fault. Well, I'm sure Detective Rhodes is on the case."

My heart winced, but I'm pretty sure I maintained a neutral expression.

"Yep, that's his job. I'd better get back to studying. Have you seen Mr. Marsburg?"

Trevor shook his head and thumped the frame twice.

"No, but that's usual. He comes and goes. I wouldn't worry about it, Eden. You've only been here a few days. You're doing great."

His beard split into a broad grin before heading down the hall-way. I stared at my screen, looking at the picture of the Youngs-town's leaving the courthouse. A sick feeling twisted my stomach as I closed my browser window. Maybe I wasn't cut out for this investi-gating thing after all.

I let out a slow breath and reopened my browser, this time focusing on my PR classes. I focused and before I knew it, Wendy popped her head in.

"Are you ready for lunch? You missed dinner last night and if you're not careful, you'll waste away to nothing. You're so tiny!"

I glanced at my watch and blinked in surprise.

"Oh geez, I didn't realize it was past noon. Thanks, Wendy. Do you have someone to cover for you while you eat? If not, I can man the desk and take my turn after you."

She made a face and leaned further in.

"Penny's got it. She's not happy about it, but what do you do? I was almost afraid to ask, given what you said this morning."

Guilt speared through me as I joined Wendy in the hall. What if I'd accused the wrong person? Now that I'd looked further into it, my convictions of the night before were fading. Fast. I tried to smile at the surly woman as we passed, but she refused to look in our direction.

We were halfway to the dining hall when I realized I still hadn't heard from Hannah. I listened to Wendy as she chattered happily about her upcoming plans for the weekend and swiped up on my phone. Nothing. That was strange. I followed Wendy into the hall and grabbed a tray, lost in thought.

"Hey! Long time no see," Danny said, bumping me with his elbow. "Glad you could join us today. What's this about Penny? Wendy was saying something earlier, but I wasn't sure about it."

Wendy shot me a guilty look before getting in line at the sandwich station. I felt even worse.

"It's nothing," I said, leaning closer to Danny. "Please don't repeat it. I shouldn't have said anything."

He shot me a curious look before shrugging, his sunny face brightening again.

"Ooo, it looks like they've got French Dips again today. You've gotta try them. They're the literal bomb."

I let him go ahead of me in the line and followed, my steps slow. The thought of eating twisted my stomach into more knots, but I knew I needed to have something. I skipped the French Dip and settled on a simple grilled cheese. Maybe some comfort food would help. I used the tongs to put some chips next to my sandwich and turned to look at the dining room. Danny was already seated and waving at me to join them. I waved back and turned, spotting Luke at the next station.

"Hey, Luke. I'm sorry I didn't help you with the cats last night. Are they okay?"

Luke shifted his lanky frame and nodded.

"No problem. I figured you were busy looking after the old gentleman. How is he today?"

"Better! The vet said he was dehydrated and severely underweight. I'm working on fixing that."

"Good, that's what Charlie said. I'm glad to hear it."

"I'll help tonight. I'd love to see the cats again."

He beamed at me and leaned across the food station.

"It's prime rib tonight, one of their favorites."

"Outstanding. I can't wait. Thanks for lending me your car, Luke. I've got some gas money for you."

"Don't worry about it," he said, waving his long-fingered hand. "I barely use the thing, anyway. I heard you got your car back."

"Yep. Still, I appreciate it."

He shrugged, blushing a deep red, and focused his attention on the person coming up behind me. I picked up my tray and walked towards the table where Danny and Wendy were eating. I was quickly learning this place functioned like a tiny, gossipy city. Good luck keeping secrets in this place.

That thought made my stomach twist again as I realized it wouldn't be long before Penny found out what I'd said. I dropped into my seat, miserable, and stared at my lunch.

"You know, typically, it's necessary to put it in your mouth to eat it," Danny said with a laugh. "Staring at it does no good. Trust me, I've tried."

"I wouldn't put it past you to absorb food, the way you eat," Wendy said. "Are you sure that's enough food, Eden?"

I nodded and picked up my sandwich. I'm sure it was probably delicious, but right now, it tasted like dust. I chewed methodically and swallowed hard. I spent the rest of the meal forcing myself to eat while I listened to Danny and Wendy. Once I'd choked it down, I hopped up, desperate to move. I needed to get back to work and stop thinking about what I'd inadvertently done.

I knew that wouldn't happen, but a girl can try, right? Danny stayed at the table, wearing a perplexed expression, but Wendy followed close behind, bussing her tray in record time and following me outside.

"Eden, wait. I'm sorry."

I turned to look at Wendy as she walked towards me, face red. I didn't have it in me to ignore her. After all, I was the one with the big mouth. I fiddled with the end of my braid until she caught up with me.

"It's not your fault, Wendy. I should've kept my mouth shut. I didn't say not to mention it, so, really, it's on me."

Wendy looped her arm in mine and put her other hand on her chest.

"Bless you, you're the sweetest thing. But I'll own this. My mouth runs a mile a minute and I rarely think about what I say. Say you'll forgive me?"

"Of course. I'll be more careful about what I say in the future."

"Well, unless it's superb gossip," Wendy said, elbowing me in the side. "I can't live without that."

I shook my head and followed her inside the resort. Penny shot me a look that chilled my liver. She may not be a murderer, but my goodness, she was unfriendly. She glanced at Wendy, raking her up and down.

"You've got gravy on your shirt. I swear, you eat like a farm animal."

"Penny!" I screeched, fiery anger rising in my chest, blotting out my remorse. "You can't say things like that."

She stood behind the desk and leaned closer to me.

"Who are you to tell me what I can and cannot do, PR girl, who doesn't even know what she's doing? That's right. I've heard about you. You can take your opinion and stick it..."

"Eden? There you are," Denise said, popping her head out of the hallway. "I need to get your paperwork done."

I never would've thought someone in human resources would be my knight in shining armor, but here we were. I patted Wendy on the arm and walked around the desk, ignoring the seething Penny.

"My office is right at the end. How was lunch?"

My shoulders relaxed as Denise led me back to her office, sat me down, and went through everything she needed. My phone rang, startling us both. I glanced at the screen and saw the caller's name.

"I'm sorry, Denise, I need to take this."

"Go ahead. I've got everything I need. If I missed something, you're just a few doors down."

I smiled and jumped up, hitting the button to accept the call on my phone before it dropped.

"Hannah?"

"Hey, Eden! How's it going?"

I blew out a deep breath before walking down the hall, popping into my office and walking around my desk.

"I've had better days. How's yours?"

"About the same. I'm sorry I couldn't call you earlier. I've got a situation on my hands, but I got that search done for you."

I flopped into my chair and waited. With any luck, she'd have the smoking gun and any vestiges of remorse I was feeling about gossiping about Penny would evaporate.

"Anything good?"

"I'm afraid not. She's gotta be one of the few people out there who have no social media footprint. She's a Valewood local, though, born and bred."

"That makes sense. Wendy said the boss's family has known her forever. Well, shoot. No sign she's a malicious killer?"

"None," Hannah said, snorting a laugh. "Sorry to disappoint."

"Well, I should've known it wouldn't be that easy. Do you have a second?"

"I've got a few minutes before an interview. What's up?"

I relayed what I'd learned about Brad and Shelly Youngstown. By the time I was done, I felt drained.

"Huh. Well, that's horrible. So, you're thinking one of the family members has a connection to the resort, and they killed her?"

I sat back in my chair and blinked.

"Well, yeah, when you put it like that, it all makes sense. I mean, it has to be someone who works here that has a motive."

"I've gotta run, but if you can get me a list of the employees there, I'll have my team start the background checks."

"Does that team comprise who I think it does?"

Hannah giggled and lowered her voice.

"Yes, they might have furry toe beans, but I will neither confirm nor deny that. They're the best investigators out there, though."

I looked at the phone for a second, marveling at the world I'd tumbled into.

"I'll see what I can put together. I've gotta see their work in action."

"If you need anything, let me know," Hannah said. "Be safe."

"You too."

She ended the call, and I kicked my legs under the chair. Somehow, Hannah tied up my thoughts in a nice little bow. I pulled up the portal to the resort and found the employee area. For a split second, I wondered if it was okay for me to access this information, but I waved off my fears. Solving this case was the most important thing right now. I copied and pasted everyone's name into an email and sent it off to Hannah.

I spent the next few hours working on my PR courses until the light coming in my window faded. I glanced up and looked at the clock. I had just enough time to surprise Jasper with his new gear before dinner started. I grabbed my coat and headed to the car, giddy at the thought of surprising my new furry friend.

# Chapter Seventeen

J asper was wide awake when I opened my door and my heart skipped when he hopped down from the bed and came to greet me.

"How are you feeling?"

"I'm not an invalid. Sheesh."

"My apologies. It's good to see you."

"Yeah, you too. Whatcha got there?"

I heaved the two bags from the pet store onto the counter and started sorting my haul. I couldn't wait to see his expression.

"I found this really cool cat tree with a comfy hammock. Look at this, it's so soft! I just need to put it together."

I knelt down and stacked the pieces next to me. Luckily, everything was numbered, and I had it assembled in no time. Jasper walked towards it and immediately sunk his claws into the scratching post, ripping with wild abandon. Dang it, I should've bought some nail trimmers. Then again, after inspecting his sabers, maybe not.

I stood back up and pulled out a few of the toys I'd found.

"I'm not sure what toys you like, so I got a bunch of different ones. See? This one is a little mouse. It squeaks when you squeeze it!"

He didn't look impressed, but I couldn't help but see the gleam in his eye when I unveiled the teaser toy. There was a brightly colored frog on the end, complete with streamers, and Jasper's eyes lasered in on it as I gently waved it back and forth.

"I'm not really one for playing," he said, tearing his eyes away. "You've always got to be on guard in the wild."

My heart sank, but something whispered inside that he just needed a little convincing.

"Well, think of it as a great way to stay sharp while you're recovering."

"But that's only going to be for another day or two," he said, stretching his back. "You really shouldn't have done all this."

"We'll see," I said, turning back to my bags to hide my expression.

He'd added a few more days to his forecast than he had before. Was he finally getting comfortable with me? I wanted nothing more than to keep him forever, but I knew he might have different ideas.

"I was going to get you a cat bed, but I skipped it since you seem to like my bed. Do you like catnip?" I asked, shaking the little bottle I'd found.

"Never had it."

"Well, we'll try it after dinner. I've got to get cleaned up. Please, play with anything that catches your fancy."

He harrumphed while I walked by, but he leaned into my hand as I stroked his head. Baby steps.

I tried to fix the fly-aways in my braid and washed my hands before peeking out the bathroom door. There was Jasper, settled into the fluffy hammock, kneading away at its side like he was a tiny kitten. I put my hand to my lips to keep my giggle silent. I knew he'd love it. I coughed to announce I was coming back. By the time I'd rejoined him, his paws were tucked underneath him, but his whiskers had a quirk that had been missing before.

"Do you want some of your wet food now or after I get back? I need to help Luke feed the clowder tonight. Oh, any messages?"

His face grew solemn, and he nodded.

"I can wait. I like to eat after everyone else has, anyway. No reason to change that. Please tell Oscar not to get too big for his britches. He'll be chafing under Fig's leadership, but deep down, he knows she's right for the job."

"Which one is Oscar?"

"Big black cat, blue eyes. He's fierce looking."

I swallowed hard. Great. I needed to put the big wild cat in his place. That should go swimmingly. I nodded, though, figuring I'd come up with a gentler way of relaying Jasper's message by the time I got to the cats.

"Anything else?"

"That should do for now. I think I'll take a little snooze."

"That's a good idea. I should be back in a little over an hour. I'll bring you back some treats."

His ears perked up, and I leaned over, planting a kiss right between them. He blinked in surprise, but said nothing. I walked over and grabbed my coat, suddenly embarrassed.

"See you later, Jasper."

"Yep. Thanks, Eden."

I grinned as I closed the door and headed to the dining hall. I recognized the bright flash of cherry red hair in front of me and jogged to catch up with Charlie. I tapped her on the left shoulder before hopping over to her right.

"Gah! You startled me," she said, putting her hand on her heart. "Hey, you never let me know what was going on today. Is Penny our killer?"

I glanced around and put my finger to my lips.

"Shhh. Not so loud. I don't think so, but I'm still not one-hundred percent sure."

"Bummer deal. I was kinda hoping it was her. So, what's up?"

I filled Charlie in on Hannah's theory as we walked inside the dining hall. A girl walked past, never taking her eyes off me, and I smiled. I didn't recognize her. I turned to ask Charlie who she was, but Charlie was already gone, jogging towards the buffet table.

"Wait up!"

"Prime rib waits for no man. Or woman. I'd forgotten that it was tonight. Oh my gosh, I'm going to eat my weight in it."

"I don't think I've ever had it. Is it a type of roast?"

Charlie let out a squeal and nearly dropped her plate.

"What? Are you serious?"

I nodded, feeling self conscious as a few people looked over at us. I spotted Danny waving wildly from our usual table and relaxed.

"I am."

"Well, those dark days end now," Charlie said, shoving her plate into my hands. "Come with me. We'll get you loaded up."

She grabbed another plate and hauled me over to the meat section. There, in all its glory, was an enormous slab of meat.

"Okay, so I know it's super pink, but that's the best way to eat it. Grab that slice there. Yep, don't be shy. Now, let me take this one," Charlie said, selecting a slice further back. "There. Now we need our potatoes, of course. Ooo, they've got smashed taters. I can't believe Danny left us some. Quick! Grab as many as you can."

I watched as she loaded up her plate, but I only took three. I piled up some steamed broccoli while Charlie shook her head.

"You're taking up valuable stomach space with veggies, Eden. We can go back for seconds, you know."

I looked at the enormous piece on my plate and raised an eyebrow.

"You'll see. Come on, let's see what Danny's up to."

By the time I sat next to Charlie, she'd already told Danny and the rest of the table about the lack of prime rib in my life. I smiled nervously as Josh, Denise, Charlie, and Danny all stared at me expectantly. I sliced off a thin bit of the meat and put it in my mouth.

"Well?"

"It's incredible," I said, covering my mouth.

I wasn't kidding. It was amazing. I barely needed to chew. I nodded my head and went for one of the smashed potatoes next. The garlicky goodness melted over my tongue. Wow!

"Ladies and gentlemen, we have witnessed history," Charlie said, holding her fork like a microphone.

I elbowed her in the side before spearing a broccoli floret. This had to be the best food I'd ever had. I munched away contentedly while everyone else talked about their day. By the time my plate was empty, I was stuffed. Even Danny had slowed down, although he was looking at the dessert section mournfully.

"I can't do it," he said, patting his stomach. "Although I could take something back to my cabin for later."

"That's what I'm gonna do. We've got that mini fridge under the front desk. There's a piece of chocolate cake over there with my name on it," Charlie said.

I groaned as I stood.

"No more talk of food. That was too good."

"Shoot, I'm gonna be late," Charlie said, glancing at her phone.

"I'll get your plate for you," I said, grabbing for it.

"I won't," Danny said, sticking out his tongue at her.

Charlie rolled her eyes before giving me a one-armed hug. She jogged over to the dessert table and snagged a plate of cake, winking as she ran past.

"Laters, Eden. You're the best."

I stowed our plates before looking around for Luke. I spotted an older woman talking to him, waving her hands around wildly. I was debating whether to interrupt them when she turned on her heel and left. I walked over.

"Is everything okay?"

Luke rubbed his forehead with the back of his hand.

"It's fine. Our dishwasher had to leave early, so I've got to stay late tonight. You don't have to wait for me. It's going to be late before I'm able to feed the cats."

"Oh, Luke. I'm sorry. I could help with the dishes."

"No, it's okay. You're not certified to run the machine."

Luke looked exhausted. He was up before the sun and worked such long days. There had to be something I could do. I tapped my finger on my lip before smiling.

"Tell you what. I'll feed the cats tonight. I know where you put their food and they've seen me before. It will be okay."

Luke's hazel eyes brightened.

"Really? You don't mind?"

"Not at all! I'll be happy to do it."

"I'll get their tray put together. Give me just a minute."

He dashed towards the back, limbs flapping, as Danny walked up.

"What's up with ole lanky man?"

"Danny! Be nice. I'm gonna feed the cats for Luke tonight. He's got to take over dishwashing duties."

"Need any help?"

As much as I wouldn't have minded company, and help to carry the heavy tray of food, Danny's presence would mean I couldn't talk to the cats. I shook my head.

"I've got it. It should only take a half an hour. Hey, where's your cake?"

He groaned and rubbed his stomach.

"I'd better not. I think I overdid it tonight. See you in the morning, Eden."

He waved as he headed outside and I turned to see Luke approached with a tray laden with many good things.

"I've found the cats actually like vegetables," he said, cheeks blushing. "They like corn and peas."

"That's wonderful, Luke. I'll be back in about a half an hour with the tray. Will the doors still be unlocked?"

"Yep. If I don't hear you, just leave the tray here and I'll take care of it. Thanks a million, Eden."

I waved off his thanks and smiled before hefting the tray. I used my back to push open the door and headed into the night. The walk seemed a little longer thanks to the tray, but the snow wasn't as soft, which evened things out. By the time I made it to the tree line, I was huffing and puffing away.

"Where's the other one?"

I gasped as I spotted Fig moving out of the shadows. Her eyes gleamed in the moonlight.

"Luke had to stay and do dishes. It's just me tonight."

She sniffed and lashed her tail. It must have been a signal, as a bunch of cats stepped forward. I spotted Ollie pacing back and forth while the smaller cats approached, their tails bushed up. I knelt and cleared off the platter Luke used for their food, speaking softly.

"Hi babies. I'm Eden. We sort of met the other night. I've got some good food for you tonight."

I eased everything over to the platter before upending it on the stack of meat so the gravy wouldn't go to waste. I watched as the smallest cats were pushed forward.

"That's right, Ember. She won't hurt you," a female cat said, her voice soft.

I smiled as a delicate ginger cat came forward. Once she reached the platter, more cats approached. I stepped back and wiped my hands on the snow before folding them around my middle. There was a definite chill in the air tonight. I spotted a black cat talking to Ollie. Was this Oscar?

Fig approached, getting closer to me than she ever had.

"Any news from Jasper?"

"He's doing better. He's jumping around and walking. He's still exhausted, though. It might be a long road to get him back to top shape."

"I can imagine," she said, eyes gleaming as she watched the younger cats eat. "Did he have any orders?"

I hemmed and hawed for a second.

"Well, there was one. But I don't know how to say it. I'm supposed to tell Oscar not to get too big for his britches."

Fig let out a cough that sounded remarkably like a human laugh, and I watched as the other cats turned to look at her. The young cats stopped eating. She waved her tail and everyone went back to what they were doing.

"Oh, Jasper," she said, purring loudly. "He knows us so well. I can relay the message."

"I'll do it. He asked me to do it personally."

She turned to look at me, her eyes speculative.

"You're more than I thought you'd be."

She walked off, tail waving, leaving me dismissed and perplexed. Did she mean that in a good way, or a bad way? I eyed the big black cat again and let him eat before I approached. A fed cat was a happy and calm cat, right? I tucked my hands into my sleeves and leaned against a nearby tree, content to watch the cats interact.

Suddenly, as one, they froze, tails held flat. Fig straightened, eyes narrow, before giving me a furious look. She gave one sharp wave of her tail and everyone melted into the shadows, leaving the food where it sat. What on earth?

"Put your hands where I can see them."

I spun around, gasping, and tried to find the person I'd heard. A tall person approached, holding something out.

"I said get your hands up!"

My hands shook as I complied. What on earth was going on?

# Chapter Eighteen

T he leaves crunched as the person walked closer to me, still holding their hand out. Did they have a knife or a gun? I wasn't sure what would be worse, but my overactive imagination was doing its best to figure that out.

"Who are you? What do you want? I don't have my purse with me. All I have is the food I brought for the cats."

"Do you actually think I'm mugging you?"

I struggled to place the voice I was hearing. It was definitely a woman, but I couldn't remember hearing it before. I needed to keep her talking.

"I'm honestly not sure. What do you want?"

She closed the distance between us and poked me in the chest with something metallic and hard. Great. It was a gun.

"I want you to stop talking."

"Okay. Done. I won't say another word," I said, miming zipping my lips shut with one hand.

Her eyes narrowed, and I immediately put that hand back in the air.

"My God, you really aren't very smart, are you?"

"Well, I wouldn't say that. I'm under pressure here and I'm never very good under pressure. I babble."

"Really? I never would've guessed."

She pushed back her hood, revealing her face. I wasn't sure what I was expecting, but she had ordinary brown eyes. Her hair was dark. Her face was round. I had absolutely no idea who she was.

"Do I know you? Do you work at the resort?"

"We have a winner, ladies and gentlemen," she said, her tone dry as she opened her arms wide.

It took me a second, but my mind finally cleared. She worked at the resort, which must mean I was facing Sherry Youngstown's killer. Unless, of course, the resort housed an entire cast of murderous characters. I pushed that thought aside and swallowed hard.

"Why did you do it?"

Her lips pulled into a lopsided smile as she bowed in front of me. I took a step back, and she immediately shoved the gun into my chest again.

"Don't even think about it. With those short little legs, there's no way you're outrunning me, Eden."

She was right. The odds of me running away were slim to none. That meant I needed to stay out here long enough that Luke would get worried and come look for me, or disarm her so I could call for help.

"You know my name, but I don't know yours."

"You seriously haven't figured it out yet? Geez, I'm wasting my time here, aren't I? Here I was worried you were going to go to the cops with everything you knew, and it turns out you know nothing. Great. Just great. If that isn't my life story, I don't know what is. Well, there's no turning back now."

My gears started whirring as the pieces of the puzzle came together. I gasped.

"You're Jemma, aren't you? Penny never sent you a message that room 413 needed towels. You set her up. You're the one who went into the adjoining room, and when the time was right, you killed her."

"Well, it looks like you're a little smarter than I thought. That's good. Now, why did I do it?"

Her face twisted into a sneer as she poked me again with the gun. She seriously needed to stop doing that. I took a ragged breath and my heart broke a little as the last piece slipped into place.

"Who did you lose in the fire?"

Jemma took a step back and angrily brushed her free hand over her cheeks.

"My mother. You don't know what it's like to lose your mother. She was my everything. She raised me by herself, working two, sometimes three jobs to keep a roof over our heads and food in my belly."

I may not have lost my mother like that, but I knew what she was feeling. The day I broke free from the cult-like situation I'd been in, my mother disowned me. It had been years since I'd seen her or my sisters. A sob bubbled up in my throat.

"I'm so sorry, Jemma."

"Oh, you're sorry, are you? Tell that to the jury who let those monsters walk. Tell that to the other people who lost their loved ones and everything they owned. They needed to pay!"

The anguish in her voice broke my heart as she paced back and forth, waving her gun. If I could just get it away from her, I could talk some sense into her.

"I agree. They should pay. I haven't lost my loved ones, not like that," I said, my voice soft as I put my hand on my stomach. "But I have lost someone. For a long time, I thought it was my fault. I should've done something differently, changed something. I blamed the man who'd left me to bear our child alone, but it didn't do any good. I agree they should pay, Jemma, but not with their lives."

"You've got a kid?" Jemma asked, her voice ragged.

"No. I lost the child to a miscarriage. The man murdered someone very close to me, the man who acted like my father should have. I'd give anything to have stopped that from happening."

I stood there, my soul laid bare, and looked at Jemma. Our eyes met in the darkness, and she whimpered, lowering the gun.

"The world's an awful place, isn't it?"

The bleakness of her tone scared me more than her anger had. I shook my head and stepped closer to her.

"No, Jemma. It's not. There are enough bright spots to light it up and chase away the shadows. No one is perfect. Nothing is. But we have to hold on to the brief flights of happiness we find. It will get better. Hope is never lost."

She raised the gun again, her hand shaking.

"I can't. I've come this far. I have to end it."

A horrible yowl split the night air and I saw a blur of brown fur streak past. Jemma's face went white, and she screamed, dropping the gun onto the leaves below. I darted forward and kicked the gun away.

As soon as Jemma registered what I'd done, she crumpled into a ball, ugly sobs ripping out of her chest. She rocked back and forth as I walked closer.

"Jemma, there aren't enough words to say how sorry I am. I know you don't want to hear any platitudes. What you did was wrong, but it's not too late. If you stop now, you can salvage it."

She wiped her cheeks and looked at me, eyes unfocused.

"I've screwed up everything. Why did you have to be so nice?"

I knelt next to her and wrapped my arms around her.

"It will be okay. We'll find you an excellent lawyer and figure it out."

"How?"

I blew out a breath and rocked back on my heels. I honestly didn't know, but I had to believe that justice would somehow prevail.

"Well, the first step is to turn yourself in. We won't mention what happened here, okay? I know the detective on the case. He's a nice man," I said, my voice hitching. "I think you'll find him to be fair. What you did can't be undone. You took someone's life. You'll have to serve time, but..."

"I didn't mean to do it," she said in a whisper. "I saw their names on the housekeeping sheet and something came over me. When I realized what I'd done, I started screaming. I tried to hide it, but I knew I'd be found out. I was cleaning Mr. Marsburg's office today when I heard you on the phone. I knew the walls were closing in."

"Well, sometimes things turn out differently than you expect," I said, standing and holding out my hand. "Come on, let's go back and we'll call Detective Rhodes. He'll know what to do."

She looked at my hand as another sob wracked her thin frame. She nodded and reached up towards me, closing her icy fingers around my hand. I knew if she changed her mind, there'd be little I could do to stop her. I just had to have faith.

"Okay."

I led her through the trees, stopping at the edge and turning back.

"Thank you," I said in a whisper, hoping Fig would hear me.

"What about the gun?"

"I'll figure something out," I said, walking forward again. "I've got to come back for the tray later, anyway."

My mind raced ahead of our steps as we made our way back to the resort.

"I don't want to see anyone," Jemma said, pulling me to a halt. "I can't handle it."

"It's okay. We'll go to my cabin."

I patted her arm as we walked through the darkened row of cabins. I wasn't sure what Jasper would think, but I didn't have many other options. I opened the door and flipped on the light. He spotted us and his hackles went up. Our eyes met and held, and he relaxed, somehow sensing what was going on.

"Sit," I said, pointing towards the chair. "I'll call Ethan."

My hands shook as I pulled my phone out of my pocket. It took me a second to realize I didn't know his number. A memory of him giving me his card flashed through my mind and I walked over to my pile of clothes, hunting for the jeans I'd worn that day. Luckily, I didn't have a washer, or I would have destroyed the card.

Jasper approached Jemma while I dialed Ethan's number, praying he would answer. I watched as the cat sat in front of her, head cocked to the side. He seemed to know she needed a friend more than anything right now. His familiar rusty purr started up as she reached her fingers towards him.

"Hello?"

Hearing Ethan's voice on the other end nearly made my knees buckle, but I held it together.

"Detective Rhodes, this is Eden. Eden Brooks. At the resort. I have someone here you need to see."

The line was quiet for a second, but I could practically hear his gears turning.

"I'll be there in fifteen minutes."

He ended the call, and I stared at my phone for a second before stowing it back in my pocket.

"He's coming. Can I get you anything?"

She shook her head fast, her short blond hair flying.

"No. I deserve nothing."

I rolled my eyes as I walked over to the kitchenette and grabbed a glass.

"Some water would probably be good. Always stay hydrated, right?"

She barked out a laugh that turned into a sob.

"Why?"

I walked over and handed her the glass.

"Why what?"

"Why are you doing this?"

"Because I believe in the good inside people. Sometimes it bites me on the rear end, but most times it doesn't."

She sipped her glass and stared at Jasper.

"Nice cat. What was that in the forest?"

I looked away, towards the door, and shrugged. I knew without a doubt Fig saved my life, but I wouldn't tell Jemma that.

"I'm not sure."

She nodded and quietly sipped her water.

"I don't know if I can do this."

"You can, Jemma. Trust me."

"I don't know you. Heck, I just tried to kill you. Why not trust you, huh?"

"We're going to forget what happened, okay? Just tell the detective you felt the need to confess to someone, and you chose me, since I'm new."

Her shrewd look met mine, and I shrugged before continuing.

"It's all I've got."

"Well, let's hope it works."

A knock at the door startled both of us and I went to answer it. Jasper stalked over to the bed and hopped on it, fur fluffed up. I opened it and met those familiar blue eyes.

"Thanks for coming, Detective Rhodes."

"Eden," he said, nodding. "What's going on?"

"Like I said, I've got someone you need to meet," I said, pointing towards Jemma with my head. "She's got something to tell you."

I sat on the bed next to Jasper while Jemma told the story. Ethan listened, sitting still as a statue. He paused and read her rights as he realized what was going on. She closed her eyes and continued talking. Even though I'd heard parts of it already, I was still moved to tears as she spoke about her mother. Once she was done, Jemma's shoulders folded, and she slumped in the chair.

"I need to take you in. Is there anyone you'd like to call?"

"I've got no one."

"You've got us," I said, standing. "I'll talk to Mr. Marsburg. We'll find you a lawyer."

She gave me a watery smile and held her hands out to be cuffed. Ethan shook his head and motioned for her to follow him. He stopped at the door, holding onto one of Jemma's arms.

"I don't know how you did it, but I know there's more to this story. We need to talk."

I shrugged, hoping my face looked noncommittal. His eyes narrowed before he prodded Jemma to keep walking. I closed the door behind them and sank down, hitting the floor with a bump. I rested my head on my knees.

I heard a soft thump and a few seconds later, whiskers tickled my hand. I smiled as I looked up and met Jasper's golden eyes.

"Alright. What really happened?"

I put my legs down and he crawled into my lap, snuggling close, while I relayed the events. Once I was done, I sat upright.

"Fig! I need to go thank her. And figure out what to do with the gun. Plus, I left the tray out there. Luke will wonder what happened to me. He trusted me to take care of the clowder tonight."

Jasper hopped down and nosed the door.

"What are we waiting for?"

I looked down at him and pursed my lips.

"It's too cold for you to go out yet."

"I'll have you know I'm made of sterner stuff than you know, little miss. Let's go."

I knew I was fighting a losing battle. I stood and gently put my hands around his middle.

"Fine, but I'm carrying you. No ifs, no ands, and definitely no buts."

He tensed before relaxing and allowing me to pick him up. I cradled him to my chest and zipped my coat up around him.

"Fine, but I'll have you know I could walk ten times as far as you could."

"I don't doubt it."

Despite his bold words, I didn't miss the way he snuggled deeper into my coat as the wind whistled past. I held him with one arm and made my way back to the forest. The path might have been flat, but by the time I'd reached the trees, I felt like I'd scaled a mountain. I took a deep breath and waited.

"You're back?"

I smiled at the familiar sharp tones of the brown cat I found sitting on a stump to my right. I hadn't heard her approach.

"Fig! There you are. I have someone who wants to see you."

I unzipped my coat and Jasper popped his head up. His golden eyes flared, and I could tell what he wanted. I carefully put him down next to his deputy.

"It's good to see you, Jasper," she said, touching noses with him. "I see you're on the mend."

A rustling sound filled the night and soon we were surrounded by glowing eyes as the rest of the clowder approached. Ollie pranced towards us.

"Jasper, old boy. How are ya?"

Jasper nodded at the rotund tuxedo cat.

"I'm well. Everyone looks good. How are things?" he asked, turning back to Fig.

She straightened and nodded at the other cats.

"Everything is running smoothly," she said, holding eyes with the big black cat I'd seen earlier.

He looked away first and Fig turned back to Jasper.

"Good, good," he said, his voice soft.

"Are you rejoining us?" Fig asked, tilting her head to the side. "The human said you need time to regain your strength."

"Now that I've seen you all, I agree with her. A few more days at the most, though, and I'll be back."

Fig's eyes met mine and something passed between us. No words were spoken, but I knew she understood me. If it was possible, Jasper would stay with me for as long as he wanted. Fig would run the clowder, and do a darn fine job at it, if you asked me. She turned back to Jasper and nodded her magnificent head.

"Good. You need to be in top form."

The cats filed past, touching noses with Jasper, twining their tails around him. My heart was in my throat at the outpouring of love from the clowder for their old leader. I waited as the last small kitten walked past, whispering her greeting. Within seconds, the only cats left in the clearing were Fig and Jasper.

"That settles it. Eden tells me you saved her tonight. You have my thanks," Jasper said.

She shrugged.

"It was the right thing to do."

"I need to find the gun and somehow dispose of it," I said, rubbing my hands together. "I don't know what to do with it, though."

"We'll hide it for you until you're ready. Get better, Jasper. We miss you," she said, her tone softening as she rubbed noses with him again.

She nodded stiffly towards me and hopped down from the stump, waving her tail. A hush descended as she left. I cleared my throat, overcome by her sweetness towards Jasper.

"Let me grab the tray and we can head back."

"Sounds good to me," he said, hopping down from the stump almost as spryly as Fig had. "You mentioned wet food earlier?"

I smiled as I picked him up and stowed him in my coat again.

"Of course. I'll just bring you back to the cabin first and then deliver this tray to Luke. I might even find you some leftover prime rib."

"That sounds good," he said, nestling close.

I grabbed the tray and started the long walk back to my cabin. My steps were lighter and joy filled my heart as I looked up at the stars. My first few days at the resort were intense, but my life was so much more full than it had been.

I'd met incredible people, started a new job, solved a mystery, and was on my way towards pursuing a degree. Oh, and of course, who could forget the whole talking to cats thing? I wrapped my arm tighter around Jasper.

"Thank you, Jasper."

"For what?"

"Being you."

His answer was a purr that I felt through my chest. A grin split my face, almost hurting my cheeks. Yep, this new life I was living was full of surprises. I couldn't wait to see what would happen next.

## Don't Miss The Next Book!

A Slippery Slope

Eden Brooks is getting into the swing of things at her new job, but not everything is coming up roses. When a ski-team books the resort for two weeks, it's all hands on deck to keep everything running smoothly.

When a member of the ski-team turns up dead, the case is anything but cut and dried. Eden's boss is the prime suspect, but he swears he's innocent. If Eden and the gang can't prove it, they'll all be out of a job, and a place to live.

Join Eden, the clowder cats, and the zany Valewood employees as they race to solve the mystery, save their boss, and their futures.

Get your copy here!

# Books By Courtney McFarlin

## Escape from Reality Cozy Mystery Series

Escape from Danger

Escape from the Past

Escape from Hiding

## A Razzy Cat Cozy Mystery Series

The Body in the Park

The Trouble at City Hall

The Crime at the Lake

The Thief in the Night

The Mess at the Banquet

The Girl Who Disappeared

Tails by the Fireplace

The Love That Was Lost

The Problem at the Picnic

The Chaos at the Campground

The Crisis at the Wedding

The Murder on the Mountain

The Reunion on the Farm

The Mishap at the Meeting - Summer 2023

## A Soul Seeker Cozy Mystery

The Apparition in the Attic

The Banshee in the Bathroom

The Creature in the Cabin

The ABCs of Seeing Ghosts

The Demon in the Den

The Ether in the Entryway

The Fright in the Family Room

The Ghoul in the Garage

The Haunting in the Hallway

The Imp at the Ice Rink

The Jinn in the Joists - Summer 2023

## **The Clowder Cats Cozy Mystery Series**

Resorting to Murder

A Slippery Slope

# Have you read The Razzy Cat Cozy Mystery Series?

### The Body in the Park
A Razzy Cat Cozy Mystery

*"I'm a cat lover and read many cat mysteries. Courtney McFarlin's Razzy Cat Cozy Mystery Series is my favorite."*

**She's found an unlikely consultant to help solve the crime. But this speaking pet might just prove purr-fect...**

Hannah Murphy yearns for a real news story. But after a strange migraine results in an unexpected ability to talk to her cat, she must keep the kitty-communication skills a secret if she wants to advance from fluff pieces to covering felonies. And when she literally trips over a slain body, she's shocked her feline companion is the best partner to crack the case.

Convinced she's finally got her big break, Hannah quickly runs afoul of a handsome detective and his poor opinion of interfering reporters. And when she discovers the victim's penchant for embezzlement and fraud, she may need more than a furry friend and a cantankerous cop to avoid ending up in the obits.

Can Hannah catch a killer before her career and her life are dead and buried?

*The Body in the Park* is the delightful first book in the Razzy Cat cozy mystery series. If you like clever sleuths, light banter, and talking animals, then you'll love Courtney McFarlin's hilarious whodunit.

*More reader comments: "The Razzy Cat series is a joy to read! I have read the first three, and just bought the fourth. These books are well written, engaging stories. I love the positive and supportive relationships depicted amongst the main characters and the cats. That is so refreshing to read. I look forward to more books in this series. I will also be reading some this author's other works. Well done, and keep writing!" - Ingrid*

Buy *The Body in the Park* for the long arm of the paw today!

# A Note From Courtney

Thank you for taking the time to read this novel. If you enjoyed the book, please take a few minutes to leave a review. As an independent author, I appreciate the help!

If you'd like to be first in line to hear about new books as they are released, don't forget to sign up for my newsletter. Click here to sign up! https://bit.ly/2H8BSef

# A Little About Me

Courtney McFarlin currently lives in the Black Hills of South Dakota with her fiancé and their two cats.

Find out more about her books at:
www.booksbycourtney.com

**Follow Courtney on Social Media:**

https://twitter.com/booksbycourtney

https://www.instagram.com/courtneymcfarlin/

https://www.facebook.com/booksbycourtneym

Made in the USA
Monee, IL
14 November 2024

70108822R00090